NUFTOOM

MOONWUFTOON

A NOVEL

BY

MARY G. THOMPSON

CLARION BOOKS
HOUGHTON MIFFLIN HARCOURT
BOSTON   NEW YORK   2012

Clarion Books
215 Park Avenue South
New York, New York 10003

Clarion Books is an imprint of Houghton Mifflin Harcourt Publishing Company.

www.hmhbooks.com

The text was set in Adobe Garamond Pro.

Library of Congress Cataloging-in-Publication Data

Thompson, Mary G. (Mary Gloria), 1978–
Wuftoom : a novel of transformation / Mary G. Thompson.
p. cm.
Summary: Confined to a bed in his darkened room, sixth-grader Evan is slowly transforming into a Wuftoom—a large, worm-like creature that lives underground—but when he is offered a chance to join forces with their sworn enemies he must decide whether to give up everything he once loved.

ISBN 978-0-547-63724-2
[1. Horror stories.] I. Title.
PZ7.T37169Wu 2012
[Fic]—dc23
2011025947

Manufactured in the United States of America
DOC 10 9 8 7 6 5 4 3 2 1
4500351744

FOR MY MOM

ONE

EVAN SAT ON HIS BED with his back against the pillow. The light was so low that the room was bathed in shadows. They fell from the clutter, making dark shapes on the worn hardwood floor. But Evan was so used to the darkness that he saw the shapes making the shadows, even the paint peeling off the once-white walls.

He saw shelves lined with books and toys and model airplane kits. Action figures sat here and there, discarded. On a rolling cart at the edge of the bed was a television. It was small and old and attached to an antenna that sat somewhere far away, on the roof of this weathered, tipping house.

His mother had boarded over the room's single window and covered the boards with a framed painting. It showed a broad meadow with tall grass, a blue sky, and sunshine his mother said was "so bright it might jump off the canvas and light up the room." Evan tried not to look at it. He would rather just have the plain brown boards.

Evan knew what was outside. It was not a brilliant meadow with tall grass. It was an unkempt front lawn, covered in dandelions. The grass was patchy, and cracked dirt showed through. Beyond the front yard was a potholed street and beyond that, the train tracks. One large oak tree broke the boredom. Its large green leaves would have just returned for the beginning of spring.

He remembered the last time he had seen it, more than a year ago. It had been winter then. The leaves had been gone, but his rope ladder had still hung from the tree trunk. He used to climb that ladder to the first fork, then climb the branches up. From there he could see more houses, more of the road, more of the train tracks. That winter he had watched the ladder through the window, straining to catch the last glimmer of sunshine, even though it hurt his eyes.

"Don't look, honey," his mother had said, placing the first board over the glass. But he had.

Evan flexed his fingers, used them to push himself up further, to a full sitting position. Moving them was like pulling a rubber band. They wanted to curl back on themselves, roll into a ball, and stay there. He flexed them more, pressed his nails against the membrane. It hurt, but he ignored the pain, flexing his fingers even harder. Then, slowly, he let them curl back, feeling the membrane relax onto itself. It felt strangely good, like poking a healing bruise.

He sucked in his breath. It came roughly, and he rubbed his nose with his fingers, upsetting the sticky membranes that had started to cover the nostrils. Rubbing them would help him breathe for a while, until they got in the way again. Without planning to, he rubbed his feet together under the blankets. The webs of the right foot grated the toes of the left. Then he rubbed the other way. It felt oddly calming and was his habit when thinking unpleasant thoughts.

He stared at the television. Inside it were a thousand worlds. Real streets, real buildings, trees, oceans, and sunshine. All that background, used to tell a story, showed Evan what was out there. Where he could be standing if he could stand at all. The TV was blank. He could watch it with the brightness turned down to almost nothing, but right now he didn't want to turn it on.

A familiar soft knock invaded the silence. Evan said nothing but stared down at his hands. He heard the creaking as the knob turned and the door slowly opened, revealing the small, partially gray head of his mother, peering in from the darkness.

The hallway was black. No light could come in from outside the room. His mother had learned to navigate the staircase and the hallway in the dark. She was carrying a wooden tray made with feet on it, for serving breakfast in bed. But breakfast was gone and this was dinner, steaming up from the plates and filling the room with its inviting smell.

Evan's stomach gurgled, and he was lifted a little from his sadness.

"Hi, Mom," he said. "What did you bring me?" He could see her smile, but he was sure that she could not see his. The room was too dark.

"Beef stew," she said, "with lots of potatoes. And biscuits!" His mother knew how much he loved her biscuits. She walked into the room, her feet tracing the path they always took, which

Evan kept free of clutter just for her. She leaned over the bed and set the tray over his legs. Then she sat down herself and closed her hand over his calf, which was underneath the blankets.

"I'm sorry it's late, honey. I had to work overtime again." Her voice sounded tired.

"That's okay," Evan said. "It's worth the wait." He bit into one of the biscuits and felt the sweet jam meld with the fluffy bread.

His mother smiled wanly. "It's Roy again," she went on. "I'm lucky he shows up at all." Roy was the person who was supposed to relieve her so she could come home and be with Evan. But he was always late.

"They should fire him," said Evan with his mouth full.

"I can always use the extra hours," she said, smiling bigger, like she wanted to change the subject. She got up and went to a shelf along the wall. She pushed her face in closely, trying to get a good look at what was on it.

"How's that model airplane coming?" she asked. She had bought him a new one, one that was supposed to be for littler kids, easier to do with his degrading fingers. His mother didn't know they were so bad now, he couldn't even do the kiddie kit.

"Oh, I didn't get to it today," he said. He shoveled the food in, hoping she wouldn't see him struggling to grip the spoon. "There were some good movies on TV."

The sad smile on her face made him unsure whether she believed the lie. He knew that there was just enough light in the room for her to see his face after her eyes had adjusted. She sighed but didn't ask about it any further.

She sat down on the bed again and started telling him about her day. The crazy customers, the stupid boss. She always injected as much humor as she could, but it still sounded sad. Evan knew that the crazy customers were mean and the stupid boss was nasty.

He knew his mother only worked there for the health insurance, so a doctor could come to Evan's room once a month, look at him, shake his head, and go away again. They had long since passed any hope of a doctor figuring this out, but the doctor kept coming.

"Dr. Allen is the best. If anyone can figure this out, he can." His mother had said this after he had returned from the hospital, after the specialists and the scientists had given up.

Evan liked the old man. He gave Evan candy and told funny stories, just like he had when Evan was very little. But Evan knew that Dr. Allen couldn't help. It was just his mother's way of hanging on to hope.

His mother stayed with Evan for a while. They talked about the movies Evan had watched on TV that week and the books he had read. With his single tiny lamp, covered so it barely glowed, Evan could still make out all the words. Now that reading was one of the few things he could do, he was starting to like it. Finally, she left the room with his dinner tray.

"Good night, honey," she said, forcing a smile as she opened the door into the blackness.

"Good night, Mom," Evan replied. As she closed the door behind her, he felt as if the darkness from the hallway sucked out what light he had left inside, even though he could still see as sharply as a cat. He felt so sorry every time she left. Sorry she had to go through having a son like this. Sorry she had to work at that awful store. Sorry she had to live alone and never get married and never have a normal child all because of him.

Evan was about to turn out the remainder of his meager light and go to sleep, the better to stop these thoughts from overwhelming him. But he heard another familiar knock. It came from inside his private bathroom, part of what once was a master bedroom. This knock was not soft. It was quiet, but it was hard. It was a knock that would not take no. Again, Evan said nothing, and slowly the doorknob turned.

He heard the shuffling of its nubs against the old wood floor. It sounded like hissing, and Evan squinted and turned his head to the wall as it came closer, not wanting to look. The hissing stopped, and that was even worse. The stink filled the room completely.

"What do you want now?" Evan asked, still looking away.

"You don't want to look at me," the thing said. Its voice was low and quiet, rough like it had a throat infection. "You are still scared of me." The thing chuckled.

"I'm not scared," said Evan. "I don't understand why you have to come here is all. Why can't you leave me alone?" He bit down on his lip and kept looking at the wall.

"To see you are well, proem, to see you are well," said the thing, with just a hint of malice.

"You *should* want me to be well!" Evan whispered. He didn't want his mother to hear, but he wanted to scream at the thing, chase it out for once instead of letting it stand there.

"Oh, I do, proem. I want you to be very well," it hissed.

"Then leave me alone! I'm getting worse anyway. Just go away and wait!" Evan hissed back, turning to face the thing at last. It was familiar, but it still always filled him with disgust.

It stood a foot higher than the bed. Its soft pink body was shaped like a finger, covered with folds of the same yellowish membrane that was slowly choking Evan himself. Its eyes were soft, glowing white balls sunk into the pink flesh. They had no pupils and never moved. Its mouth was a tiny wrinkled hole, deep in the thing's face. Only when it opened in laughter could Evan see the two sharp fangs. It had no nose.

Its shapeless, fingerless arms were attached to its body by folded fanlike lengths of membrane. They were touching each other in grotesque imitation of clasped hands.

"Getting worse, proem! I am so sorry to hear you speak this way of us." Its tiny mouth widened in a toothless smile.

"I'll never be one of you," said Evan, glaring at the thing, willing himself not to be weak, not to look away again. "I might look like you, but I won't go with you. I won't live like you in the sewers. I'm going to stay with my mother. She'll take care of me." Evan flexed his fingers, feeling how they still separated, still pushed against and stretched the membrane.

"The sewers are only temporary, proem, only temporary," it said, rubbing its stumps together. "We'll live like kings soon, in the other dark places." The thing seemed unconcerned that

Evan refused to ever go with it. Each time Evan made this statement, the thing would ignore him and talk of how much better the future would be. And it seemed like the more it talked, the more it stank.

"There are places you would never go as a boy, proem, places you have never dreamed about. We'll go there together, you and I and our brothers."

Evan had heard it all before. A paradise underground, made for things like the worm in front of him. A place where Evan would forget he had ever been human, forget he had a mother, maybe even forget his own name. This thing did not remember its own, Evan was sure of it.

"I'm still a boy," said Evan, glaring straight at it. "I'll always be a boy, even if I have a worm's body. You're just a man with a disease, even if you don't know it."

The thing widened its mouth, rubbed its nub arms harder. "Boys play outside, proem," it rasped. "Boys go to school. Boys spend their time with other boys. They prepare to be men. But you do not prepare. You wait."

"I may not go outside or go to school," said Evan a little louder, "but I *will* be a man someday. I'll be strange and disgusting and I'll never see anyone but my mother, but I'll still be a man!"

The membranes surrounding the thing's body rippled a little as it leaned forward over Evan's bed. Its stink got even worse as it moved closer. "Proem, proem," it rasped. "You are healthy, you are healthy!" Before Evan could stop it, the creature had pushed the blankets back with its nub arm, revealing Evan's membraned fingers. The thing pointed its sunken white eyes toward Evan's face.

Evan twitched his nose under the thing's gaze, and the membranes flapped lightly. They not only covered Evan's nose, but they also hung down from his eyebrows and seeped onto his cheeks. Evan knew what "proem" meant. He had asked the thing the first time he had seen it. It meant larva. That was what Evan was to them.

It seemed so long ago that the thing had first come, explained to Evan what none of the doctors could, what was really wrong with him. Evan had been scared but strangely relieved to have an answer at last. When Evan had asked how he'd caught it, the creature had laughed. A loud, gravelly, hearty laugh filled with malice.

"How did he catch it, he wants to know!" it had chortled. "He thinks he has a disease! Something he catches, something he cures. Oh no, proem, you are not sick."

"I'm not sick? How can I *not* be sick?" Evan had screamed at it. The membranes had already been growing fast.

"You do not remember," said the thing. And then it had told him. It had laughed as it told, showing its sharp fangs, pursing its shriveled lips in satisfaction.

"You must have a cure! Give it to me!" Evan had begged.

"Oh no, proem," the thing had said. "You came to us. You have us in you, and we can no more stop this than your mother could stop you from growing in her womb."

Evan had asked Dr. Allen, was it possible to catch something like this? Could he not be dying at all but be turning into something else, like a caterpillar turns into a butterfly? *Only the other way around,* Evan had thought. "Oh no," said Dr. Allen. There were no diseases that did that. It wasn't possible. You couldn't turn into a completely different creature. Evan had been grateful that the old man hadn't laughed at him but had pursed his thin lips seriously before he answered.

As he remembered the past, the impossible future stared up at him, smiling with its shriveled hole.

"Get away from me!" said Evan loudly, pushing the thing backward with one hand. It stumbled for a second but then regained its composure and its nasty smirk.

"For now, proem, for now," it said. "I will check up on you again." Still smirking, it shuffled back into the bathroom. Using both nubs, it pulled the door closed behind it. Its stink did not leave with it, and Evan knew it would fill the room for hours.

He slept fitfully that night, like he always did after a visit from his future kin.

TWO

THE SUN WAS BRIGHT on his frayed shoes. Too bright. He stepped out onto the sidewalk and looked both ways. The town was deserted. No one was behind him. No cars were on the streets. The streets glowed with too much light, as if the sun were also burning from below the ground.

Evan burned with it. Blood-boiling, skin-frying, eye-popping anger pushed him forward. He strode down the empty sidewalk, around a corner, and down the road. The houses got thinner and the yards got bigger. Instead of blocking the light, the trees magnified it, so that every branch created glare rather than shade. The heat from inside him sizzled the concrete beneath his feet.

He kept walking until the yards turned into fields. Manicured lawns became expanses of tall grass, stock-still and shining in the dead-calm day.

Suddenly, a chain-link fence appeared, rising high over his head. It cut off the field and stretched beyond the eye into the forest, which started at the edge of the field and thickened over low hills. Evan tromped up to the fence through the tall grass and gripped it with both fists, staring through the wire past the brown grass, into the evergreens. It seemed like a forest of pure light.

Next to his hands a large wooden sign hung, peeling faded yellow paint. PRIVATE KEEP OUT, it said, in once-black letters.

He lifted his hands to grip the fence higher, placed one foot on a low link and then the other. *No! Don't do it!* a voice screamed. But he didn't seem to hear it. He climbed swiftly, throwing himself over the top and landing softly on the ground. His anger had changed into excitement, and he walked swiftly toward the glowing forest. His feet pounded the solid ground, and the ground lifted each foot for its next step. *Stop!*

His foot landed in something soft, and sank. Deeper and deeper into the pit. A sweet stink rose up and around him, and, suddenly, the sun went down.

Evan started awake. It was the same dream. Over and over and over again he dreamed it. He dreamed it often alone, and always when the worm was near. He pushed himself up, straining against the membrane. It was getting harder every day to sit up straight.

The sun had not been so bright in real life, nor had it cut out when he had walked into their trap. A few cars had rumbled down the country road. The grass had swayed softly in the breeze. He'd landed so hard after jumping off the fence that he'd screamed over his burning feet. But the essence of the dream was true. He had walked away from school on a bad day. No one had noticed him except to knock him out of their way. No one had noticed when he left.

He had climbed the fence because he could climb. It was one thing he could do better than the other kids. If climbing were a team sport, he would have been a hero. He had done the one thing he could do, and now he could do almost nothing.

In every dream he screamed at himself to stop, and every time he went on climbing, excited and oblivious.

He had struggled in the sweet pink goo, flailing with his arms, pushing with his free leg. He had pulled himself out and slowly wandered home, oozing a pinkish trail like slug slime.

Until the worm thing told him, he had never connected the pink goo with his illness. It seemed obvious in hindsight, the way the itching had spread from his leg to his whole body. How the light had burned on that leg first, and then the wind. How the membranes followed the itching, attacking his left side first. But it hadn't been obvious to him, nor to the doctors who had poked and prodded him.

He was in the hospital when sixth grade started, grateful to be missing it. He didn't have to brave the hallways of the middle school, where he'd be picked on by even more boys, sighed at by more teachers, and ignored when he wasn't being picked on. He had figured that the longer it took the doctors to cure him, the better it would be. It was several months before he realized they would not cure him.

Evan remembered everything he'd hated about school. The other kids. Reading aloud in class and being laughed at when he stumbled. His old clothes and free lunches. Never being noticed. He thought about recess, sitting alone under a tree. It had made him so angry then.

That night his mother's soft knock came again.

"Ready for dinner, honey?" she asked, peeking her head in. She was trying to sound bright, but Evan could tell that, as usual, she was dead tired.

Evan ate and listened to his mother talk. He couldn't stop thinking about school. What was it like? What were the other kids doing? He wondered what the popular kids were doing, the ones who had picked on him or, worse, ignored him. He desperately wanted to see their faces, to go back to the time when he had sat there in the back of the class and envied their every move. Evan hadn't talked with his mother about this for a long time because he didn't want to make her sad, but tonight he couldn't help it.

"Mom," he said quietly, "I miss school."

If he had said this two years ago, his mother would have laughed and asked him if he was sick. Tonight she just looked down at him. "I know, honey," she said.

"I miss going outside!" he cried, suddenly loud. "I miss playing basketball and getting left on the bench! I miss getting grapes thrown at me in the cafeteria! I miss getting my report card with all Cs and Ds!"

His mother reached over to hug him.

"Don't!" he cried. "What if it's catching?" His mother had hugged him a thousand times since he'd gotten sick. If she was going to catch it, Evan knew she would have. But he couldn't think straight. How did he know the goo only worked if you stepped in it? What if his body was producing goo without him knowing it, and everyone he touched would turn into a worm too?

"Oh, honey," his mother said. "I don't think it's catching. I don't care anyway." And she reached down and hugged him.

Evan couldn't help himself. He felt the tears start to roll down his cheeks. They caught and puddled in his membranes.

"I'd give everything I have to make you well again," she said tearfully. "I'd do anything God asked if He would cure you." She hugged him tighter, so that his strangely shaped internal organs groaned inside him.

"I want to be alive again! I feel like I'm already dead." He sobbed. And his mother sobbed with him until they couldn't cry anymore.

THREE

THE NEXT MORNING Evan lay on his bed, eyes sore. He stared up at the ceiling, the way he had spent so many days. He had counted the cracks and made up stories about them. They were a map of an alien planet, a puzzle sent for him to solve. If he could go to the planet or solve the puzzle, he could get out of here, he would imagine. Now he saw them as just cracks in an old house that was falling apart.

He stared at the light fixture above him. It hadn't been used since before he got sick, when this was his mother's bedroom. The light it gave off was too bright now. It would burn him, melt his newly membraned skin.

As he stared at it, it began to move. Just slightly, as if shaking in a mild breeze. Then came the sound. *Scrape, scrape, scrape.* Evan's heart beat loudly and he stared harder. The fixture was opaque white. He could see a shadow inside it. The shadow was so big that it was hard to make it out at first. It nearly filled the fixture, but he saw it flutter. *Scrape, scrape, scrape.*

"Who's there?" Evan called softly.

Scrape, scrape, scrape.

"Are you trapped?" Evan pulled himself up. His skin groaned with the effort.

"Let . . . me . . . in." The voice was shrill, inhuman. It made Evan's blood freeze.

"What do you want?" he whispered.

"To talk to you, proem," the voice said. "To make a deal. To help you if you help us." It was not a worm speaking; that much Evan could tell. A worm couldn't fit in there.

"What are you?" he asked.

"I am something else that lives in darkness. I am an enemy of the worms. We will help you if you help us." The strange voice was still chilling. But Evan had heard its words.

"What do you want me to do?" Evan asked.

"Let me in, proem. Let me in and we will talk." Its voice was too strange. There was something wrong about it. He did not want to let it in. He took a deep breath, which nearly made him cough. An enemy of the worms.

"All right," said Evan. "I'm going to unscrew the fixture."

The thing fluttered and the fixture clanged.

"All *right,* I'm coming." He stood up on the bed and reached his arms up. A pain ripped through his stomach like a knife blade turning, and he gasped. He grabbed on to the fixture with both hands and twisted slowly. At least his hands could still do this.

The fixture fell suddenly, and something flew at Evan's face. He ducked quickly, swallowed a scream, and fell backward onto the bed, curling into a ball. His stomach burned.

Evan stared upward, into the glowing yellow eyes of a giant bug. It was a foot long from wingtip to wingtip. Its wings were black and so shiny they might have been made of a plastic tarp, except for dull patches that looked like hair. Its large yellow eyes were round with a tiny dot of pure black pupil. They sat at the front of its face and stared back at Evan with a light that seemed to come from far within. It had two sharp fangs that looked exactly like the fangs inside the worm's mouth. Above each fang was a large patch of coarse black hair.

The bug's slit for a mouth widened into a kind of smile.

"I hope I have not frightened you, proem," it said.

"Don't call me that!" Evan cried, trying to sit up straight on the bed and not look scared.

"It is not what you want to be, but it is what you are." The thing's voice softened into a hiss.

"You're right!" cried Evan. "I don't want to be one. You said you could help me, so talk." Evan tried to look it in the eyes. Their brightness hurt him, but he didn't look away.

It fluttered its wings, then set down on the bed in front of him. The ends of its spindly legs were equipped with narrow, sharpened claws.

"You want to go back to school," it hissed. "You want to go outside. To feel the sunlight, feel the breeze."

Evan felt ashamed that the bug had heard him crying. But it was true. "You said I'm a proem," said Evan. "That means I can't go to school and I can't go outside. Unless you can cure me?" Evan allowed himself to hope. But the bug shook its hairy head.

"No, no, proem. Trust me, we would cure you if we could."

"Well, how can you help me, then?" Evan sighed, turning away.

"We cannot cure you, but we can take you away," it hissed. "For a while, proem. So you can see what you are missing."

"What do you mean?" asked Evan.

Just then something fell from the open light fixture onto the bed, landing with a soft plop. It fell right between Evan and the bug. It was square and thin and made of wood, not much bigger than Evan's hand. Evan reached down and picked it up. When he brought it up close to his eyes, he could see that it had etchings on it, but they didn't seem to be in any pattern.

"What is it?" Evan asked.

"It is a gateway to the world, proem," the bug said. "When you have given yourself to it, it will take you into the world of the minds. They are all connected, you know, all the minds of all those things that have them."

Evan didn't know. He stared at the bug blankly.

"You feel all alone, you humans. You think no one understands you. But you are closer to others than you think." The bug blinked for the first time. Even its eyelids appeared hairy as they slowly closed over the yellow eyeballs and opened again.

"You mean there's another world?" asked Evan. "A place where I can live without my body?"

"Oh no," said the bug, "the world of the mind is like a web. It connects your minds to one another like your computers are connected to each other."

"So, I can go into this web and outside somehow?" Evan asked.

"You stay here in this room," said the bug. "And your mind

travels. To whoever you would like to visit. Whoever you would like to be."

Evan thought about this. "I can go to someone else's body?" he asked finally.

"Anyone you like," the bug replied. Its fangs pulled up slightly and then extended down again.

Evan's mind raced. He could be anyone! He could walk around outside. Go to school. Go wherever he wanted! "For how long?" he asked. "Is there a limit?"

"For as long as you are human," said the bug. This sobered Evan up. Two years ago it would have been a joke. It would have meant forever.

"And how long is that?" Evan asked fiercely. "You know what I am, so you must know how long I have."

"I do not know for sure, proem," the bug said. "Longer than tomorrow, but not more than a year."

"A year?" Evan cried. He was sure it was much less. "Don't you know better than that? Look at my hands!" He held them in front of the bug's eyes. "Can't you tell me what this means?"

"All proems are different," said the bug. "But you have been human a long time."

Seeing he could get nothing better from it, Evan clenched his fists and pulled them back. The membranes liked the clenching. They tightened happily around his fingers.

"My name isn't proem," said Evan. "It's Evan. Do you have a name?"

The bug screeched, a high-pitched, wailing, awful sound.

Evan covered his ears.

The bug opened its mouth in a wide grin, making the hairy part above its fangs nearly rub into its yellow eyes. "That's how we say it," it said. "You may call me what you want."

"Foul," said Evan, without thinking.

"I like it," the bug hissed.

"But what do you want?" Evan asked, remembering, turning his head away. "You said you wanted a deal. That you'd help me if I helped you."

"We are a race that lives in the dark," Foul said. "We are one of many races. There are things that crawl and things that fly. Things that talk and things that only mutter. The worms are another race like us." Foul's fangs moved up and down a little as it talked. Its shrill voice was quiet and serious.

Evan sat silently. His heart pumped.

"We eat them," Foul said. "And they would eat us—if they could." The thing let out a screeching chuckle.

Evan shrank back from it and pulled his hands under the blankets.

"Don't worry, proem," it hissed. "We do not eat proems. They are still human in their way."

"Do you want to eat me when I change? Give me my life back in exchange for taking it later?" Evan cried. "I won't do it! Take it back!" He picked up the square of wood and held it out so that it nearly touched the bug's face.

"Oh no, proem. You shall walk away a free worm if I have anything to do with it. If you perform the little service that we ask." Its wings flapped. Evan set the object down again and pushed himself backward, as far as he could, into the wall.

"What little service?" he asked, his voice barely coming out.

"When you change over, they will come for you. They will lead you to their home. It is down in the sewers, guarded by falling water, which they know we cannot pass through. Yet we are sure there is a dry route in. Or, if not, a way to force them to come out. You will help us find it. You will help us eat them."

Evan stared at the bug, speechless. "You want me to help you eat them?" he asked finally.

Foul slowly blinked again. "Help us destroy them, proem," it said. "There will be no more like you. No more children stolen. You will be free."

"If there are no more of them, won't you starve?" asked Evan. He thought the creature was trying to trick him, to make him feel like he would save others when it wasn't true.

Foul chuckled, a strange vibration of its belly that came out as several squeaks. "There are other creatures in the darkness who taste just as good. But they are weaker and would not destroy us."

"You want to kill every single one," said Evan. Why did this bother him so much?

The creature's fangs grew. Its smile was as much like the worm's smile as an expression could be when made by a creature shaped so differently.

"I'll still be one of them. I don't like it, but I will be!" Evan said, not believing he had said it.

"You have vowed never to go with them," Foul said. "I heard you speaking with it. It wanted you so badly, I could smell it."

The bug suddenly raised its two front legs and rubbed them together, making a faint humming sound.

"I hate them," Evan said. He stared down at the wood square. "How does it work?"

"You put your hand on it, stretched out flat. It will enter you and pull you out."

"And into someone else's mind?"

"You will be able to travel. To look and to choose." Foul put its front legs down and moved forward almost imperceptibly.

Evan looked down at the wood square, half believing, half not. Did he care about the worms at all? Would he be better or worse off without them, once he'd turned?

Foul seemed to be reading his thoughts. "I am giving you a chance at life," it said, moving just a little closer. "You can be the other boys and also save them from your fate."

Evan thought about the school, the picture he had made up in his mind. It seemed to sparkle in the sunlight. The boys and girls walked happily up and down the hallways, their hands and feet flexible and normal. They stood perfectly straight. They laughed and chatted and were light and free.

"Try it," Foul squeaked. "Try it and decide."

Evan picked up the wood square with his left hand and looked down at it. It seemed like the scratches on it had a pattern after all, but he still couldn't make out what it was. He looked at the bug, who had slid even closer, so that the light from its eyes lit up the wood.

He took a deep breath and put his right hand on the square,

stretching his fingers out as best he could. It felt too cold. He and the bug stared at each other for a few long seconds.

Suddenly, the wood became hot. It was so hot that Evan tried to jerk his hand back, but he couldn't. Frightened, he tried to shake it off. It was stuck to his hand like glue. It began to mold around his hand, no longer like wood at all.

Foul continued to stare at him, its fangs shaking slightly.

"I don't want to try it anymore!" Evan cried. "Make it stop!" But the bug just stared at him and shifted even closer. The square now covered his hand and started growing up his arm.

"Make it stop!" he cried again. He reached out for the bug with his left hand, but it lifted itself off the bed and out of reach. And then Evan was gone.

FOUR

H E COULDN'T SEE OR FEEL anything but lightness. A scary, unbelievable lightness, like he might float into space. His body was gone, and with it the membranes tugging, breath wheezing, head pounding. He was free! But the absolute darkness was like nothing he had felt before. He seemed to be expanding. Expanding and expanding and—

What do I do? he thought, desperate for someone to hear him. *How do I get back?*

A voice came straight into his mind, with almost no pause. He wasn't sure if he even heard the words, or if he just knew their meaning.

Go where you want to go, proem, it said. *Wherever you want to go, you will be there.*

Evan tried to close his eyes, but nothing happened. He had no eyes to close. He thought wildly. School. He wanted to go to school. He thought it so hard he imagined he was shouting.

Suddenly, he saw light. It surrounded him and blinded him. For all he knew, he was in the middle of the sun. But, slowly, the light became manageable. He was not in the middle of the sun at all. He was hovering over the new middle school, staring down from some invisible place in the air, watching the people file in.

Evan had been there once. There had been a grand opening. In front of the large, double-doored entrance he now looked down on without eyes, the chairman of the school board had given a speech. Evan hadn't listened. He had stared at the doors in fear like they were a gateway to hell.

The doors looked shabbier now, but there was nothing demonic about them. They swung open and shut with the stream of kids, who were talking and laughing loudly. The sun was still shining brighter than he had ever seen it. The sky was bluer and the grass was greener. He searched the crowd for anyone he knew, eager to try out the creature's gift.

How do I do it? he thought. *How do I get in someone?*

Direct your energy, Foul's voice hissed. *Direct it all at one child. He will not be able to stop you.*

Evan searched. The kids ran by so quickly that he couldn't catch their faces. He didn't know anyone, and soon the crowd thinned. It was almost eight o'clock. Evan had just decided he would have to pick someone, anyone, when he saw the face of somebody he knew. The kid stumbled out of a car and raced across the sidewalk toward the steps. Evan didn't have time to think about "directing his energy" before he jumped.

He felt like his head was being clamped down with a vise. What had been free was now contained. Compressed into a too-small space. The boy felt it too. He stopped on the steps and bent his chin over his chest, slamming his eyes shut. The motion of the head made Evan feel worse, and he could feel the body around him, holding him in. Fear rose up, and Evan wasn't sure if it was his fear or the boy's. He felt the boy's heart racing, blood pumping. Their hands twitched.

"Cory?" a voice said. It sounded adult. "Cory, are you all right?" Evan felt a hand on his back. On Cory's back. He wanted to jump, but inside Cory, he went nowhere.

Cory stood up straight again and opened his eyes. Evan looked through them, right into the dark brown eyes of a young man who was stooped over and staring at him.

"Yeah, I'm okay, Mr. Houser. I don't know what happened." Cory sounded confused.

"Are you sure?" asked the teacher, still with the concerned look.

"Yeah, thanks, I'm gonna be late," said Cory, and he continued running up the steps and through the double doors. The movement caused Evan to toss inside. He couldn't see straight out of Cory's eyes but saw from one angle one second and another the next, like he was bouncing against springy walls.

He tried to steady himself but kept falling from one side to another. He caught glimpses of the hallway as Cory ran, strange pieces. A metal locker here, a square of ceiling there. He struggled and struggled, but he couldn't stay straight.

Cory barreled around a corner, pushed his way into a classroom, and sat down with a heavy sigh. His backpack dropped to the floor with a loud crash.

"Tardy, Mr. Parker," said a woman's voice. As Cory sat still,

Evan managed to settle down, and then he looked straight out of Cory's eyes. He saw a tall, stern-looking woman standing behind an overhead projector, glaring at him.

"Sorry, Miss Andrews," Cory panted. Evan felt the breath in Cory's body, moving in and out in shallow pulses.

The class was pre-algebra. Evan didn't even know what algebra was, but that didn't matter. While Cory listened to the teacher and scribbled in his notebook, Evan pressed himself forward, trying to see everything that he could out of Cory's eyes. As he did so, he felt Cory's hands moving, his body rustling in the chair, the way he squiggled his toes inside his boots.

From the farthest point he could reach, Evan looked around the room. He noticed other kids he knew. They looked different, some of them very different. Many he didn't recognize at all. He took in everything. Their faces, their clothes, the books, the windows that mottled the bright sunlight.

Cory went to the next class, and the next, and Evan took everything in. He concentrated on what Cory was feeling, how his legs and arms moved as he walked down the hallway, how his eyes blinked.

As Cory made his way to the cafeteria and stood in line, Evan felt the buzz of all the kids around him. There were so many. He couldn't make out any voices, and it was far too loud.

Cory picked up his tray and turned to face the room. The tables seemed to go on for miles. Kids were standing and sitting and yelling. Evan wanted to cover his ears, but Cory just walked out there, winding among the tables. Finally, he sat down in an empty spot, a little way from the nearest kids.

Evan pushed himself to the front of Cory's eyes, trying to see where Cory wasn't looking. After a minute he was able to see those sitting near him. He recognized some of the group. In fifth grade they had been some of the most popular kids. And from the crowd gathered around them and the way they were laughing, it looked like not much had changed.

Cory pretended they weren't there and continued eating, but Evan was fascinated. He had never been able to stare at them as much as he wanted.

His gaze fell on their fingers, curling around their forks as they ate, separated and unwebbed. He wanted those hands. Cory stopped eating for a second. This distracted Evan, snapping him back into Cory's sight line. Cory turned his head toward the popular kids.

"What are you looking at?" asked one of them. It was Jordan Bates. Jordan had been on Evan's basketball team. While Evan sat on the bench, Jordan had played almost every game. He had been taller than Evan and had blond hair and blue eyes. Now he was even taller. He looked down at Cory.

"Nothing. Sorry," said Cory. He turned back to his food.

"Freak," said Jordan. The other kids laughed.

Cory tensed up but kept on eating.

From the edge of Cory's eyeballs, Evan watched the group. There was Angela Owens, the prettiest girl in his fifth grade class. She had her hand on Jordan's leg. There was Andy Meyer,

Jordan's best friend. He recognized a couple other boys and another girl, but there were strange faces too.

Suddenly, Evan remembered what the bug had said, that he could choose.

How do I do it? he thought. He waited a moment, but Foul didn't seem to be there. He pushed himself to the far edge of Cory's eyes. Cory was still looking down at his tray, but Evan had a good view of Jordan, who had forgotten all about Cory and was laughing with his friends.

Jordan, thought Evan. He leaped through the air, expanded into the space, then was compressed and trapped by the firm grip of Jordan's skull. Andy was in front of him, slurping milk from a carton. Angela was next to him, so close it made him want to jump. Cory was rubbing his temples like he had a sudden headache.

From inside Jordan, Evan could see that Cory was dressed badly. His clothes looked old and didn't fit well. His hair was a little long and greasy. After he was done rubbing his head, he hurriedly picked up his tray and walked away. His ratty, untied bootlaces flopped on the floor. Evan didn't remember Cory looking this way before and wondered what had happened to him.

"What a freak!" said Andy.

"Yeah, why was he staring at us?" said another boy. His name was James, Evan remembered, but he didn't remember much about him. He had a long, thin face and dark hair and eyes. Evan couldn't remember ever speaking to him before.

"Oh, stop. He didn't do anything," said Angela.

Jordan laughed and mimicked her. "Oooh, stooop!"

"Shut up!" she cried, punching him.

Jordan felt different than Cory had. For one thing, he was bigger. As Jordan stood up with his tray, Evan felt himself expanding, filling the excess space. As he looked down on the table, it was farther away.

Instead of trying to see out, Evan concentrated on being Jordan. He felt his hands on the tray, grasping only lightly. Jordan handled it carelessly, swinging it into the tray tower with one hand. When he turned around, his friends were all behind him, still laughing with each other.

Evan had never had this many friends around him in his life, but this was obviously normal to Jordan. He put his arm around Angela's shoulders and led the other kids outside, where they all sat down on the grass and went on talking.

"There's that freak again," said Andy, picking up a small rock. He threw it at Cory, who was making his way around the track, bootlaces still untied. Cory appeared not to notice the rock, even though it whizzed in front of him.

"Hey, Cory!" shouted Jordan.

Cory looked up cautiously. Evan could see on his face that he wanted to ignore it.

"Come over here." Jordan waved his arm, beckoning Cory.

Miserably, Cory walked slowly over. "What's up, Jordan?" he said, looking down at his shoes.

"Nothin', man, just wanted to say hey," said Jordan. Andy and James and the other boys snickered.

"Oh. Hey," said Cory, still looking down. Evan had been on

the wrong end of this before. Somehow, Jordan and his friends could make you feel like they had beaten you up just by talking to you.

"That's all," said Jordan.

Cory turned around and shuffled off, not back to his slow walk around the track, but inside the school.

Evan felt sorry for Cory, but his new senses overwhelmed his thoughts. The breeze rolled over Jordan's skin, cool and pleasant. The sun lit up the sky and the sharply colored grass. As Jordan and his friends laughed, Evan smiled inside, sucking the world in. He thought nothing could get better than this.

"See you at practice," said Andy, getting up from the grass.

"Later," said Jordan, also standing. Evan wanted to jump with excitement, so much that he rolled inside Jordan and nearly spilled out into the air.

Basketball! Jordan was the best on the team! He sat through Jordan's classes, shaking in his new skin. He heard nothing the teachers said, saw nothing but himself tossing the ball into the hoop.

FIVE

EVAN JUMPED AND TURNED and tossed and ran like he'd never done any of those things before. Jordan never seemed to get out of breath. Even before his illness, Evan had always gotten tired quickly. He had watched boys like Jordan in amazement.

"We're going all the way this year, I can feel it!" said Jordan, and Evan felt the same excitement coursing through him.

"All the way!" echoed Andy.

All the way! thought Evan. Imagine winning the state tournament! Evan had never won anything in his life. Evan's excitement continued through Jordan's shower, until Jordan reached the parking lot outside the school, where his mother was waiting to pick him up.

Evan thought he was through the best part of the day and was about to go into the boring part. The part where Jordan went home, had dinner, did his homework, and went to bed. But then Evan saw Jordan's mother's car.

It was a black convertible. Evan didn't know anything about cars, but he knew this one was fancy. It must have cost more than Evan's *house.* And Jordan's mother was just as amazing as the car. Where Evan's mother had graying hair and a face filling with lines, Jordan's mother still looked young. She had short, bleached-blond hair and was wearing a formfitting dress that draped gracefully over her knees.

If Evan had been himself, his mouth would have dropped open. Jordan tossed his bag into the back of the car and jumped into the passenger seat.

"How was practice today, honey?" Jordan's mother asked.

"Great!" said Jordan.

"You'll have to tell your dad about it," she said, laughing.

Evan felt the wind in his face as they drove home. It felt exactly the way that wind should feel.

Jordan lived in the nice part of town. There weren't many truly rich people in town, but Jordan's parents were close. Compared to Evan's run-down house, Jordan's looked like a mansion. It had three stories and the outside was freshly painted. The yard was perfectly manicured. Jordan's mother pulled into a huge two-car garage.

A few minutes later Jordan's father came home. He was a big man who looked much like Jordan, except his blond hair was streaked with gray.

"Hey, buddy," said Jordan's father, clapping Jordan on the back. "How was practice?"

"Great!" said Jordan, and he launched into a detailed explanation of who had done what and how well or badly they had done it.

Evan had never met his own father, at least not when he was old enough to remember. Jordan came home every night to one.

Even the dinner at Jordan's house was better than dinner at home. Jordan's mother had made some kind of white fish, which was covered in a nutty crust. Evan couldn't remember the last time his mother had made fresh fish, and when Jordan took a bite, Evan savored it.

Eagerly, he waited for Jordan to take another bite. But Jordan didn't seem to like the fish. He scarfed down a baked potato covered in sour cream and butter. Evan liked that, but it was nothing compared to the fish. Evan even wished Jordan would touch his broccoli, because it looked so much better than the frozen kind his mother made.

As Jordan reached for another potato, Evan still wanted another bite of fish. *Eat the fish!* he thought.

Suddenly, Jordan abandoned his potato and took a huge bite of the fish. He put almost half the remaining fish in his mouth at once. Bones dug into Jordan's cheek. It was so much fish that he could barely chew it. Jordan's mother stared at him.

"I thought you didn't even like fish!" his mother exclaimed. She had her napkin settled primly on her lap and sat up very straight.

"Mmmhgl," said Jordan. He made a great deal more noise in a frantic effort to pull out all the bones.

Evan felt Jordan almost choking, but in his excitement, he barely noticed. He had made Jordan eat the fish!

Just as he realized what he'd done, he wondered how late it was and looked down at Jordan's watch. It was almost 7:00 p.m.! His mother would be home any minute and find him . . .

How would she find him? She might be home already. Evan had no idea what had happened to his body while he was gone.

Home! Evan thought frantically. *Back!*

Then he was being sucked away. It was much faster than how he had gone out, so fast that he barely felt the space. He was sucked back into his body, felt the vise on his head and the weight of being twisted and clamped.

He opened his eyes to the dimness of his bedroom. Foul was still sitting in front of him, staring with its glowing eyes. Evan watched it dully, letting the weight of being in himself sink in, every pain and every ache.

"Did you enjoy yourself, proem?" the bug hissed.

"You knew I would," said Evan. He was angry at the bug for using him, but he knew he couldn't give up what it had offered. If he could get out of his body, even for the short time he had left, he had to do it. The wood square lay silently between Evan and Foul, looking every bit as shabby and useless as it had when Evan had first seen it.

"Then I will see you when you turn," Foul said. Its fangs opened into a smile, and flapping its wings quickly, it rose up into the light fixture and was gone.

Evan stared after it for a second, then stood up on the bed to replace the fixture. His stomach burned again. The fixture was heavy and his hands were even tighter from not being used. It took him several tries and a long ten minutes to get it screwed on right.

When he was done, his body curled back on itself as he sank down onto the bed, aching and burning and breathing hard.

It felt even worse now that he had played basketball as Jordan Bates. He wanted to cry, but he had to hold it back because his mother was knocking at the door, carrying a tray full of her cooking.

Yesterday dinner had been the bright spot of his day, but today it seemed bitter and poor.

SIX

THE NEXT DAY, Evan didn't wait until school started. As soon as his mother had said goodbye, he pressed his hand to the wooden square and was enveloped by it. He sailed across town in the darkness, floated through the walls of Jordan's house, and found Jordan upstairs, brushing his teeth.

With a whoosh and a clamp, he was inside Jordan again.

Jordan's hand jerked a little as Evan dropped in. He swore and licked the toothpaste off his lip.

"Jordan! Are you ready?" called Jordan's mother from downstairs.

"Coming!" yelled Jordan, and he bounded down the stairs two at a time, Evan bounding with him.

The rest of that day, Evan practiced. He knew he could affect what Jordan did; he just needed to figure out how. It turned out to be surprisingly easy. Evan just had to concentrate on Jordan doing a certain thing, and Jordan would do it.

While Jordan was taking a multiple choice test, Jordan started filling in A. But Evan concentrated on B, and Jordan erased A and filled in B. As soon as Evan stopped concentrating on it, Jordan cursed to himself and went back and filled in A again.

As Jordan was walking toward a class, Evan concentrated

on turning around and heading back down the hallway. Again, once Evan stopped concentrating, Jordan turned around and went back the right way. While Jordan was in class, Evan practiced tapping Jordan's feet and cracking Jordan's knuckles.

During lunch Evan practiced taking food he wanted to eat. Jordan spluttered on milk he hadn't meant to drink, choked on chicken he hadn't meant to eat, and spat out pie he didn't even like.

"What's wrong, dude?" asked Andy, laughing at him.

"Nothing!" cried Jordan, choking on his milk again.

Evan laughed inwardly. He could do this to everyone in the school, one by one, if he wanted to. And no one could do anything. If he'd had more time, he would have done it. But he was sure the bug was wrong. His body wouldn't hold out for much longer. He wanted to be normal again, for however long he had.

"The food sucks is what's wrong," said Angela, picking up a grizzled piece of chicken with a fork and eyeing it. "I think the milk is sour." She picked up the milk and sniffed it.

"Yeah," said Evan, with Jordan's voice, "the milk's disgusting." Jordan closed his mouth and looked around him. "What the—" Evan cut Jordan off and clamped his mouth shut. Jordan opened his eyes wide and looked at Angela, shaking his head wildly.

She pushed herself back a little bit. "Uh . . . are you gonna barf or something?" she asked.

"No!" said Evan, far too loudly. "I'm fine. Sorry." He turned back to his food and started eating again. This time Evan kept the concentration on. He ate the rest of the lunch in the order he wanted to eat it. He could feel Jordan somewhere behind him, but as long as Evan kept concentrating, he couldn't get out.

After eating, Jordan's group went outside again. Evan tried to mimic how Jordan would talk. He got some funny looks, but all of Jordan's friends stayed with him.

He remembered where Jordan's next class was, so he walked his body down the hallway. He still marveled at how tall Jordan was, and how much stronger than Evan. Where Evan would have gotten knocked into and pushed over, Jordan could just walk around. Evan strutted down the hallway, never moving out of the way for anyone.

It took a lot of work to concentrate like that, and Evan wasn't going to waste his energy on *this* part of school. When they got to class, Evan released Jordan and relaxed back.

Jordan jumped like he'd been electrocuted. Then he groaned and put his head in his hands. Everyone in the class looked at him.

"Hey, man," said a boy near him, "you all right?"

"I'm fine," Jordan snapped. Some of the kids snickered. Jordan, who obviously wasn't used to being laughed at, whipped around in his chair to see who it was. That just made them snicker more. Jordan turned back around, red in the face with anger. Evan felt his muscles tense.

For the rest of the day, Jordan barely talked to anyone. His nerves leaked into basketball practice, and even though Evan enjoyed it, it wasn't the same. Jordan stomped toward his mother's car.

"How was your day, honey?" asked his mother.

Jordan was quiet for a second. "Mom . . ."

"What is it?" she asked.

"Have you ever felt like . . ." He paused, and his mother looked at him strangely. "Like someone else was inside you pulling the strings, like you didn't have any control over what you did?"

His mother paused thoughtfully. "Well . . . I guess so," she said. "I guess I've done some things I wish I hadn't done. Did something happen today?"

"No," said Jordan, "I mean . . ."

What was Jordan going to say? "I missed a lot of shots today. I was just really off!" said Evan. This time Evan didn't give Jordan a chance to come back and act crazy. But Jordan didn't make it easy for Evan to hang on to control. He was struggling inside his body more than ever. Evan's mind pushed him violently back.

Jordan's mother cooked chicken for dinner that night, and it was a lot better than the chicken Evan's mother cooked. Evan slowly savored every bite, ignoring Jordan's angry pushing. Both of Jordan's parents looked at him strangely, but Evan didn't care. He was Jordan Bates, the most popular kid in school, and he could do what he wanted!

SEVEN

THE NEXT MORNING, Evan caught Jordan when he was already in the car with his mother.

"Are you sure you're all right?" she asked.

"Yes!" cried Evan. "Did I say something was wrong?"

His mother twisted her eyebrows. "Are you having . . . you know . . ." She trailed off and looked straight at the road ahead.

"No," said Evan. "It's nothing like that." He wondered what problem Jordan possibly could have. Maybe he wet the bed at night, Evan thought, grinning inside.

"You know you can talk to me about it if you are," she said. But she looked stiffly ahead at the road and her fingers tightened around the wheel. Evan didn't think she wanted to talk about it any more than he did.

Evan decided that when he got home, he would take apart Jordan's room and look for evidence. Maybe he would write something in ketchup on the walls. Then his parents would really think he was losing it. Evan snickered at the thought.

At school, Evan bounded around, now fully into the role of being Jordan Bates. He greeted Jordan's friends and apologized for yesterday's practice. When people brought up things Evan didn't know anything about, he just pretended he wasn't interested in the subject. He was sure that was what someone as stuck up as Jordan would do.

He even started paying attention in Jordan's classes. Unfortunately, he hadn't taken over any of Jordan's reading ability. Even after all his time in bed, he still read painfully slowly. At least in seventh grade, teachers didn't make you read out loud. Besides, what did he care? They were Jordan's grades. Jordan probably had enough As to last a lifetime.

And the best part, the part Evan hadn't even imagined, was that Jordan Bates had a girlfriend, who even after two years was still the prettiest girl in school.

At first he felt just as nervous as if he were still Evan, the boy who had never spoken more than two words to the fantastic Angela Owens.

Before lunch, Evan went to the boys' room and looked in the mirror. He had looked in the mirror as Jordan yesterday, but today he took a long, hard look.

Jordan's blue eyes stared back at him. His perfectly mussed hair stuck up in just the right places. His clear skin almost glowed, especially when compared to the zits that peppered Evan's face beneath the growing membranes.

Someone called out to him as he left the bathroom, but he ignored it. All he could think about was getting to Angela's locker.

She was with one of her friends when he walked up. Evan didn't recognize the girl, but she was almost as pretty as Angela. Angela had long dark-red hair that fell around her shoulders in perfect curls. She had blue eyes the same color as Jordan's and a perfect button nose. The other girl was blond and a little shorter, but she also had blue eyes and perfect hair. They giggled together as Jordan walked up.

Angela hit him in the chest.

"Hey!" Evan exclaimed.

"That's for not calling me!" she cried, but her voice didn't sound too angry.

"Hey, uh . . ." Evan scratched his head. It had never occurred to him to call her. Shouldn't Jordan have done that after Evan left?

Angela rolled her eyes at the blond girl.

"Hey," said Evan, waving at her. He figured she must be a friend of Jordan's too.

"Hey," said the blond girl, beaming at him.

"I'm sorry," said Evan. "My mom was on the phone all night."

"Your mom was on your phone?" Angela gaped at him.

Evan suddenly realized that Jordan must have a cell phone. *Of course he does,* he thought. He kicked himself.

"It's broken," said Evan.

"Oh," said Angela. She grabbed his hand and started walking toward the cafeteria.

Evan nearly fell over. He had never held a girl's hand before. He could feel his palm starting to sweat. *She'll know,* he thought wildly. But he followed her. By the time lunch was over, he was even talking to her in an almost normal voice.

That day practice was canceled, so Evan let Jordan go just

long enough to call Jordan's mom. When she got there, she still looked worried, but she didn't say anything about the morning. As soon as he got the chance, Evan bounded up the stairs to Jordan's room, resolved to dig up Jordan's secret. But as soon as he saw the room, he forgot all about that.

Jordan had a large flat-screen TV in his bedroom and fancy speakers for his iPod. Evan didn't know much about TVs or speakers, but he knew fancy. Jordan also had the newest PlayStation and the newest Xbox. Evan had an old PlayStation at home, but he couldn't play it anymore.

Evan looked down at Jordan's hands and grinned. As fast as he could, he turned on the Xbox and started a game. It took him a few minutes to figure out how to get the whole setup going and he wasn't any good at it, but it didn't matter. His fingers moved across the buttons like a skipper bug on water. He had thought he would never be able to do this again.

All at once, he started crying. Tears flowed down Jordan's pale, perfect face and ran onto the controller. Jordan's body shook with sobs. *I might have one more day,* Evan thought. *Maybe two days. Maybe a week.* Longer than tomorrow, but less than a year, the bug had said. And tomorrow had passed.

Jordan's mother appeared in the door. She looked down at him, and she was crying too. Evan didn't know why Jordan's mother was upset, but he let her sit down on the floor next to him and put her arms around him. Right then it didn't matter why.

EIGHT

WHEN HE SAW his own mother again, Evan was silent. He felt like he had been crying, but his face was dry. He couldn't move much, nor did he want to. While she talked about her day, he stared at the wall.

Pictures of Angela punching him, Angela smiling, Angela grabbing his hand, ran through his mind. And then there was Jordan's bedroom. Jordan's mother. Jordan's blue eyes and blond hair in the mirror. Jordan's unwebbed fingers.

Evan's mother didn't ask what was wrong. *She thinks she knows,* thought Evan. *She thinks I'm just sad because I'm getting worse.* Dully, he wondered what would happen if he told her. Would she laugh? Or cry? Or would she have been through so much that she would just sit there and let it go?

He slept that night, but when he woke up, he felt no better. It was a worthless, restless sleep. He sat in his bed, wanting to be Jordan, but not wanting to, because he'd just have to give it up again and be *this.*

When he finally jumped, it was after breakfast time. Jordan was already sitting on the staircase, his shoes untied and his head buried in his hands. Evan remained there. *Why can't I just be happy?* he thought. *Why can't I enjoy it while it lasts?* He felt a presence standing over him. It was Jordan's father, dressed in a suit and tie, looking down at him gravely. Evan looked up.

Jordan's father was a tall man. Stocky, but still in good shape. Evan knew he was some kind of bigwig who worked at one of the banks on Main Street.

"Jordan," he said. "You have to go to school. You can't stay home. You're not sick."

Evan looked up at him, unsure of what to say.

"This business about being possessed. I have an acquaintance who's a psychiatrist. I'll make you an appointment."

"I don't need a psychiatrist," said Evan, alarmed. But Jordan's parents couldn't really do anything, could they? He tried to smile, wondering how Jordan looked.

"Do you think this is a joke?" asked Jordan's father. "Why won't you talk to us?"

Evan looked down at his feet. Jordan's father sat down below him on the staircase. He sighed and looked a little kinder. "Your mother and I are still dealing with it too, you know. You're not in this alone." He patted Jordan's knee.

Abruptly, Evan got up. "Go ahead and make the appointment if you want to," he said. Jordan would probably need it once Evan was gone. He brushed past Jordan's father and out to the car, where his mother was waiting in silence.

Evan had thought it would get easier, but Jordan was pushing him harder than ever. It was all he could do just to walk straight. Angela was waiting at Jordan's locker. She looked pale and worried.

"Jordan, is that you?" she asked.

"What do you mean? Of course it's me. I don't look that bad, do I?" asked Evan, trying to sound normal.

Angela looked shocked and took a step backward. Too late, Evan realized that Jordan must have told her. Did they have a code word? What could it be?

"What's wrong?" he asked.

Angela shook her head, turned, and ran down the hallway away from him. Looking around, he realized everyone was staring at him.

"Guess she's mad at me," he said with a forced smile.

A couple kids laughed, but most gaped at him like he was a moron.

He stalked off to his first class in an even fouler mood, thrusting Jordan deep inside him. It seemed like fewer people were talking to him than normal. Nobody passed him notes or whispered to him in class. By lunchtime he was boiling with anger. Why were people treating him like he was Evan?

Outside the cafeteria, he confronted Andy. Andy was supposed to be his best friend. The number two to Jordan's number one.

"What's going on?" Evan asked loudly. He poked a finger into Andy's chest. "Why is everyone ignoring me? Did Angela say something to you?"

"'Why is everyone ignoring me?'" Andy mimicked. Someone behind him laughed. Suddenly, he felt surrounded. All of Jordan's lunch group had gathered around, except for Angela, who was nowhere to be seen.

"What's your deal?" he said angrily.

"'What's your deal?'" Andy mimicked back. "What's wrong with you?" His voice was disdainful. He pulled his head backward as if Evan smelled bad.

"Look, uh . . . Angela ran off this morning. I'm sorry if I've been distracted."

Andy kept looking at him like he stank. The others had the same look.

"Whatever," said Evan. He turned and pushed his way through all the watching kids and headed back inside the school. He heard footsteps behind him and turned. It was Cory Parker. "What do you want?" Evan snapped.

"Don't let them bother you," said Cory. "They'll get over it."

Evan stared at him. "Cory, why are you being nice to Jordan Bates? He's always treated you like crap." Then he realized what he'd said. "I mean . . . I . . ."

"You're not that bad! I mean . . ." Cory looked scared.

"Oh, hell." Evan punched a locker. It made his hand sting, which made him even madder. "I'm not Jordan Bates."

"I should have said this before, but I'm really sorry about your brother," said Cory.

Evan stared at him. "What happened to Jordan's brother?" he asked. He didn't care if Cory thought he was crazy or not. He wasn't going to be Jordan anymore.

"My dad was in a car accident when I was little," said Cory. "He almost died, too, but he lived and now he's in a wheelchair."

Evan vaguely remembered this. Cory's father was bitter and mean and a drunk. No one ever saw him, but everyone knew.

"Jordan's brother died in a car accident?" asked Evan.

Cory gaped at him.

Evan hadn't even known Jordan ever had a brother. But that explained why Jordan's parents had thought they understood. Suddenly, Evan thought about what his mother would do when he was gone. It wasn't the first time he'd thought about it, but it seemed more real for some reason.

"Bye," said Cory, and he rushed off, down the hallway and away from both Jordan and the other kids. His bootlaces were tied today, but his clothes were shabby and didn't match.

Evan jumped out of Jordan and hovered above him for a second.

Jordan flinched, jerked his arms into the air, and looked around. He looked down at his hands and made two fists, then released them. He stared back at the door to the courtyard, where his former friends had been. Then he turned and followed Cory in the other direction. Evan saw him turn off into the boys' room.

Evan floated through the doors and back outside. His mind expanded into the air, and it calmed him. He could see 360 degrees. The grass, the kids, and the school were below him, while above him the sky was blue with only a pair of large gray clouds. He rose higher and floated over the town. He tried to shut out his thoughts, to let himself expand and feel the lightness of not being trapped in any body. He stayed there as long as he could, until the sun was nearly gone and the town glowed with electric lights.

NINE

IT WAS EVEN HARDER to open and close his hands. The membranes on his face were thicker. His breathing was labored, and he had to constantly brush his arm across his nose to keep the nostrils open. He wondered if he was getting worse because his body had been sitting still for days.

He tried to act happy for his mother, but his mind wandered. To basketball. To eating food as Jordan Bates. To opening and closing his mouth without feeling it slowly tightening, shriveling into the withered hole of the worm's face.

It did not help when the worm thing showed up that night. It slid into the bedroom late, when Evan was finally about to sleep, nub legs scraping sickly.

"You have had a visitor," the thing rasped.

Evan said nothing and turned his head away.

"You do not have to admit it. I know."

Evan still said nothing.

"Our enemy has offered you the world. It has offered you a life, of sorts. But at what price, proem? Are you not aware that you are faster becoming ours?"

Evan was not looking, but he knew the creature's fangs were showing as it grinned.

"Wouldn't you have done it if you could?" Evan asked softly.

The thing ignored his question. "Our enemy believes it is clever," it said. "But it is not more clever than we are. We will use its bribe against it and come out ahead."

Evan smelled it coming closer. "I won't help you any more than I'll help the bug thing," said Evan. "I won't help either of you."

"You will help us," the creature rasped. "Or you will pay the price." It nearly spat the last word at him.

"What price could I pay?" he cried, as strongly as he could while still keeping his voice down. "Will you turn me into a fruit fly? Will you kill me? I'd be better off if you did!"

"Our enemies are anxious things." It smiled at him. The fangs shook, deep inside the withered hole. "When you have not led them to us as you promised, they will not care how hard you've tried. They will be glad to have a meal."

Evan felt a chill run through him as the image imprinted on his mind. The image of Foul's sharp fangs, joined by a hundred others. Screeching. He tried not to show his fear, but the worm creature missed nothing.

"So we will use this gift it has given you," it said with its fangs showing. "Do you remember where our trap is, proem? The one you so nicely wandered into?"

"No," said Evan.

The worm ignored him. "You will bring more children to it." It chuckled to itself, a harsh sound with no warmth. "You will walk them into our bodies, the remains of our lost brothers."

Evan had suspected what the goo was made of, but hearing the truth was still horrible. He turned his head away again and stared intently at the wall.

"Or you'll feed me to the bugs," he said bitterly.

"They will have you without our protection, no matter what they promised," the worm replied. "Help us and you live, help them and you die. Bite by bite." The thing chuckled again.

Evan knew it was true. He knew that Foul was not trustworthy. He had known that when he took its offer. But how could he do it? How could he force other kids into his own fate?

"You will do this in the morning, proem. We both know you are short on time. You will bring us all that you can manage in a day, and tomorrow when the sun goes down, I will meet you back here for your change. It is almost time to bring you home."

"No!" Evan cried, so loud it echoed in the room. "Not tomorrow! I need more time!" Evan burst into tears. He felt the salt water dripping down his cheeks. It caught in the membranes and stuck there, collecting like rain on an old tarp.

Two doorknobs turned at the same time, one creaking in sorrow, the other in glee.

His mother poked her head into the room. She was wearing a thick old flannel nightgown, ragged at the ends like it had dragged a thousand times across the floor. Her hair was messy. Strands fell limply over her eyes. She looked afraid.

Evan looked up at her. "I'm sorry," he sobbed.

His mother sat down next to him and rubbed his back. "It's okay, honey," she said. "Did you have a nightmare?"

Evan forced himself to calm down a little bit. "Mom . . . I didn't have a nightmare," he said finally. "Don't ask me how I know, but I do. I'm not going to be here tomorrow night."

She looked at him sadly. Evan thought she must be too tired to freak out. Too tired to cry. She sighed.

"I'll call Dr. Allen tomorrow," she said.

"No," said Evan, shaking his head. "You don't understand, Mom. I'm not going to die from this. I'm changing into something else." He paused to see what she would say to that, but she just kept looking at him tiredly. "I know Dr. Allen says it's impossible, but what does he know?"

"He knows that you're going to get better, Evan." She smiled at him, but only with her mouth. She was trying so hard to make it a real smile. "No one is giving up on you." She removed her arm from his back and gripped his leg with her hand, over the blankets, looking him right in the eye. "I promise."

Evan put one of his membraned hands over hers. He wasn't going to hide it anymore. "I'm turning into something like a worm. It's like a giant worm with fangs. I've seen one. They live in the sewers. They're coming to get me tomorrow night, so I can go and live with them."

Tears shone in his mother's eyes. She searched his face. "Why are you saying this?"

He couldn't tell her the rest, about Foul and the wood square, and Jordan Bates. "Because it's true, Mom. It is."

She was silent for a long minute. "You're right," she said finally. "Dr. Allen doesn't know what's wrong. I don't know if what you're saying is impossible or not." She put her other hand on top of his. "You really think it's true, don't you?"

"Yes," said Evan. He looked away from her but then looked back. "I don't know if I can come back or not. If I can't handle the sun now, or the wind, or even electric light, then what will happen to me when I change? Maybe I won't be able to come up aboveground at all." He thought about the one that visited him, but he didn't want to get her hopes up. He also didn't want her to see him like that.

His mother searched his eyes silently. Evan saw her eyes change, saw that she finally believed him. Tears began rolling down her face. "You'll try, won't you?" she said. She put her arm around his shoulder and pulled him close.

Evan wasn't crying anymore. He loved his mother, but he wished she'd let him go. He wished she'd go back to bed. He wished he'd never told her anything, so he didn't have to face this. He sat there numbly, but his mother didn't leave. She stayed with him all night, first clutching his body, then holding his membraned hand.

It was all Evan could do to get her to go to work in the morning instead of staying with him. He told her he was exhausted, that he needed to sleep. That it would happen even sooner if he didn't sleep. It wasn't a lie, he knew. He wondered if by staying in his own body, he could put it off for one more day. Wouldn't the worm scream when it saw how it was cheated! But the image of the bugs stopped him. Bearing down with their fangs drawn, their wings covering the sky.

TEN

JORDAN WAS STANDING at his locker with Angela. They were talking in low voices, their faces nearly touching. Jordan had to bend down to reach her. His hair was disheveled. Angela's face had a scared look. Jordan's face was pale, and he had dark circles under his eyes.

Evan was sorry. He was so sorry that he thought he could feel his own heart, beating inside Jordan's as he jumped into Jordan's body. *But I don't have time to be sorry,* he thought.

He turned Jordan's body around and ran. Angela screamed after him, but he didn't stop. He dodged the waves of students, knocking into several, and burst through the front doors.

Jordan fought hard. There were no words, but there was anger. It boiled through Jordan's body, and Evan barely maintained control.

He ran into the street, as fast as Jordan's strong, athletic legs would take him. Rain pelted his body, but he ignored it. The houses got thinner and the yards got bigger, until the yards turned into fields.

He was soaked through, but he didn't stop until he reached a tall chain-link fence with a faded yellow sign that said PRIVATE KEEP OUT.

Evan stared through the fence and across the field. He was

breathing heavily from running, and from the fight that was going on inside.

He wasn't sure exactly where the goo was, and the field was bigger than he remembered. The rain had changed everything. Pools of mud and water filled every dip. Had he walked straight into the middle, or had he veered off to the side? The grass was tall, and anything in it was hidden from view. But he didn't have time to waste. He had to just go look for it. He grabbed on to the fence and started to pull himself up.

But Jordan's body was different from Evan's. He was too big, not skilled enough at climbing. The water didn't help him. His feet slipped from the wires and he fell back to the ground, nearly twisting his ankle and covering himself in mud.

Evan thought back to when he had climbed the fence as himself. He tried to remember how it had felt. How his hands had moved and where his feet had planted. He tried to expand inside Jordan. He had been controlling Jordan's movements, but his primary focus had been on Jordan's mind. Now he moved down, into the rest of Jordan. He pushed his focus into Jordan's muscle and bone, replacing Jordan's feelings with his own.

He jumped onto the fence again. This time he was able to hang on. He wasn't as good as when he'd been Evan, but he clambered up and dropped heavily over the top into the mud.

Suddenly, Jordan turned back to the fence. He grabbed on to it with both hands and began pulling himself up again, then slipped and dropped back to the ground.

Evan pushed back into Jordan's head, willing to take control again. But Jordan fought him more than ever. Their minds thrashed around each other. Without real muscles, there was only will. And Jordan's fear rose to Evan's desperation.

I'm going to be eaten! Evan thought. *I'm going to die!*

Something came back from Jordan, but there were no words. It was a scream in Evan's mind that vibrated through him into their shared skull.

Jordan's body turned toward the field, back toward the fence, then back again. He stopped with one hand on the fence and the other reaching away from it, like two giants were pulling on his tiny arms. His face was tightened in a grimace.

I am not going to die! Evan thought. He threw himself, whatever he was, against his rival. They knocked around inside the body, mixing with each other in a vapor of steaming souls.

Jordan fought hard, but Evan had more experience. Just as Evan would have no chance in a basketball game, Jordan was no match for an experienced body stealer. Evan turned and tore and thrust Jordan away.

He let go of the fence and ran the body through the grass, faster than he had ever run. In the middle of the field, he turned and looked wildly around him. Where was it? He ran to the left, then to the right. Where was the puddle deeper? Where was the mud pink?

Jordan was still pushing. Evan couldn't hold on for much longer. Then he saw it. A faint pink glimmer to the left and back, toward where the field met the forest. He ran to it and nearly pitched over the edge but pulled back from it just in time, staring down into the pit.

How could he *do* this? No one deserved this! *But they'll eat me!* he thought. *They'll eat me alive!*

Jordan pushed, thrusting Evan down into the body. Jordan whipped around too quickly. His feet tottered on the edge of the pit and his arms waved. Evan thrust himself into Jordan's brain, but it was too late. Jordan fell backward into the goo.

Evan watched from above as Jordan rolled over onto his stomach and tried to push himself up, his hands sinking in deep. His feet were still partly free, and he kicked them as he squirmed. He finally turned himself face-up again but was now totally covered in the pink goo. Evan was sure that he would sink, not having both hands and a leg free as Evan had, but Jordan was strong.

On his back, he pulled his arms up sharply until they were free. Then he reached them out to the banks of the hole and pushed with both his hands and feet. When his back was almost free, he pushed with his right hand and threw himself up onto the ground where his left hand had been.

He lay in the mud, panting and crying.

Evan felt sorry. Jordan had no idea what was about to happen. And he was no more deserving than Evan. All the jealousy seeped away from him as he looked down. Now Jordan was just like him. Another proem.

The rain washed off some of the goo. It separated on the ground into pockets of pink. The water seemed to run off it, leaving it pure. Jordan lifted himself up and looked around.

Evan rode with him as he walked, not interfering until Jordan needed a little bit more skill to climb the fence. He felt the weight of the soaked jeans, the increasing chill as the rain dripped through to Jordan's skin.

Jordan walked back to the school, becoming even more soaked with each dejected step.

Evan left him before he reached it. He could not go back to school. He could not do this to anybody else. He let his consciousness drift to the ground, almost into a puddle on the sidewalk. He had no idea what to do.

The worm would be angry, Evan thought, and it would threaten him. But surely it wouldn't kill him? Surely it wanted him too badly. It was logical, but the more he thought about it, the less he was sure that the creature worked by logic. Sinking further into the ground, he knew that he should not have taken even one other kid.

He thought of Jordan's mother. How would she react when her son began to fall ill, after just having lost another?

It doesn't matter, Evan told himself. *It's my last day on earth. It doesn't matter what happens now.* He wanted to stay there on the ground, sink into it, and never go back to himself. He would expand and drift into nothing. It would be better than becoming a worm.

He would have done it, but there was one person he still cared about.

ELEVEN

HE FLOATED INTO THE STORE. It was the end of her shift, but there was still a line at the register where his mother stood, scanning items, taking money. She looked exhausted. Her graying dark hair was pulled back into a messy bun, with pieces falling everywhere. It looked like she had slept on it, but Evan knew she hadn't slept.

A customer wanted to chat, but Evan's mother only gave a sad little smile, and the customer went away again, replaced by the next one and the next.

Evan jumped into a man as he was handing his mother a twenty-dollar bill. He was a burly man, stout and strong and tall. He looked down on his mother's graying head. Evan had never seen her from this angle. She seemed smaller. For the first time in his life, he didn't see her as his mother, but as a person. A worn-looking woman who was much too young to look the way she did.

Without really looking at him, she took the cash. There was a tension as she pulled it, as if she wanted to pull harder. As if she wanted to rip the bill in two and everything else with it. She slowly put the bill inside the drawer and gave him the change back, still not really looking at him. He tried to catch her eye, but she looked down.

"Tough day?" Evan asked. He cursed himself for saying something so ordinary, but it was all he could think of.

His mother forced a tiny smile and tapped the fingers of her right hand shakily against the counter. "You know, same old." She glanced up at the clock, wiping a stray hair out of her face with her left hand.

"Roy late again?" asked Evan.

His mother squinted at him. "Do I know you?"

"I come here a lot," said Evan. He noticed that his mother was wearing a name tag. SHARON, it said.

His mother shrugged. Her eyes were wet, and now that Evan was really looking, he could see that they were bloodshot. "Yeah," she said. "He's late."

"They should fire him," said Evan.

His mother smiled, her eyes lighting up a little bit. "That's what my son says." Her smile faded again. She chewed her lip and looked down at the counter, fingers still tapping.

"Hey!" a lady behind him said. "Are you done?"

Evan moved out of the way. The man was pushing against his mind, but he couldn't let him go just yet. He moved over to the magazine rack and picked up a newspaper, still watching his mother out of the corner of the man's eye.

"You know people are waiting, right—Sharon?" said the lady, slamming a Diet Coke down on the counter. There was no one behind her.

"I'm sorry about that," said his mother.

Evan watched the struggle of his mother's hands as she stuffed the lady's wrinkled bills into the rusting cash register.

Her hands shook, and she looked up at the clock again. She was obviously trying not to cry—over him. Why had he told her what was happening to him? He could have waited until the very last second, at least spared her a little bit of this.

The lady left, leaving the store empty except for Evan and his mother. His mother wiped a tear away, then glanced at him, then looked down, wiping her eyes fiercely.

Evan had forgotten who he was in. This strange man must be making the situation even worse. He jumped out of the man and hovered in the air above the magazine rack.

The man looked around him, put down the newspaper, and headed for the door. As he pushed the door open, he bumped smack into Roy.

"Watch where you're going," said Roy. He was tall and thin, except for a potbelly that stuck straight out from his middle, and older than Evan's mother. "Hey, Sharon."

Without thinking about what he was doing, Evan jumped into Roy. Suddenly, he had a close-up of his mother's face.

"I am so sorry," said Evan. "I know what I've put you through." He stopped, closed Roy's eyes, remembered who he was in. "I know how much it means to you to spend time with your son. I promise it won't be a problem again." He wanted to reach out and put his arms around her, but he knew Roy couldn't do that. He had to stand there, watch her try to hold the tears back.

"Goodbye, Roy." She grabbed her purse from under the counter and rushed out, not looking behind her.

Evan jumped out of Roy and followed her.

She slid into her dirty old station wagon and peeled out of the parking lot. She was crying freely now, speeding and careening around corners.

Evan wanted to cry too, floating inside the car, rolling with the turns. Which would be worse for her? he wondered. Having him here, or having him gone?

As she pulled into the driveway, Evan slid back into himself. He tried to lift his head, but it barely moved. While he had been out of his body, his head had lolled forward and the membranes had grown from his chin into his chest. As he struggled to move, they stretched only a little. His webbed hand lay, twisted, on the wood square. From the way his fingers were now curled, he knew he would never be able to open them well enough to use the square again. And a thick membrane had grown down from his nose, sewing his lips almost completely shut.

The light fixture fell from the ceiling and landed on Evan's leg. He yelped. It was a strange sound, weak and whiny. He could not look up, but he didn't have to look to see what had fallen with it.

"Running children into their trap, proem," Foul hissed. "Shall I *trust* you? Shall I presume it *forced* you?"

"It was only one," Evan whispered. His voice was barely audible and garbled by the membrane. "You should be happy. It's just more for you to eat." Evan heard its wings beating the air.

"Never mind what they have offered. Or what they have *threatened*. You will meet us here in this room, at this time, three weeks from now. You will deliver on our bargain. Or it will not be just you who we tear into, piece by piece, then bone by bone." Its wings flapped harder. "We don't like to eat humans, but we can." The sound of its wings flapping rose up and up, and with a sucking noise, the thing was swallowed into its hole.

Without knocking, his mother burst into the room. Her tears were worse than just a few minutes before. And then she really saw him.

"Evan!" she cried, and raced over to his bedside. She tore the blanket away from his body and sobbed over him. His legs were now fused together, too, the thick yellow membranes like plastic tubing, not flexible at all like the webbing of his hands. His toes were curled under, and the membranes glued them to the bottom of his feet. "It can't be true. Don't go yet!"

"Don't . . . watch . . . this . . ." he growled, but it came out like a painful squeak. His mother just went on sobbing. Tears fell from Evan's eyes and filled up the membranes covering his face, so it looked like he was in a fish tank.

"I love you," he squeaked. "Please don't watch."

His mother stared at him. "I love you!" she sobbed, and she threw her arms around him, squeezing him tight. Some of the tears escaped the membranes at the top of Evan's cheeks and dripped down onto her head. She kissed him on the head and, with one last squeeze, ran shaking from the room. She slammed the door behind her, and Evan heard her drop down on the other side, shaking the door frame with her sobs.

TWELVE

EVAN TRIED AGAIN to move his head, but it was still stuck to his chest. A few tears were trapped between the membrane and his skin, or what was once skin, and they tickled him. He flexed his cheeks to move them, but they wouldn't go.

His organs twisted and heaved, sliding around his body and tearing the tissue as they slid. They had shifted slowly over the years, so that Evan was not sure where his liver, kidneys, or stomach were. His heart was near the center of his chest now, and his lungs . . . he had no idea where they were. He seemed to be breathing from his whole body at once.

He tried to scream in pain, but his mouth was nearly pulled shut, and nothing but a hum came out. He jumped like a suffocating fish, flopping on the bed, reaching his hands toward the cracked ceiling. But a force greater than Evan's pulled them down again and wrapped them to his flopping body.

All at once, the membranes beneath his chin softened and his head popped back from his chest. He was staring at the ceiling, but the picture was distorted through the growing membranes. They covered all of his face and were thick over his eyes. As soon as they had let his head up, they reworked themselves and extended from his chin to meet the membranes that grew quickly up his neck. As they met, he was immobilized again, like a long, stiff Popsicle stick.

His hearing suddenly became much more acute. He heard his mother sobbing from behind the door so loudly that she might have been right next to him, sobbing into a megaphone next to his ear. He tried to cry out again, but his mouth was still too tightly shut. The rustle of his sheets as he tossed and twisted was as loud as the banging of hundred-foot sails in a storm.

He would have covered his ears, but his arms were pinned, and the sound seemed to come into everywhere at once, ringing his toes as much as his head.

Then all the membranes on his body tightened. They wrapped and squeezed, and Evan flopped and tugged, but it was useless. He was stuck, folded in a little, now more like a banana than a Popsicle, staring up blurrily at the light fixture that was now a gaping hole. He wondered if Foul was up there in the darkness, looking back at him, salivating. He tried to close his eyes to keep from looking up, but they wouldn't close. The membranes squeezed even tighter, and his whole body gasped for air. He sucked with his nose, but nothing came in through the mask. His blurry eyes got blurrier, and then, for a second, it all went black.

He came to with a deep breath. Like the sound, the air seemed to come in from all over, as though his whole body was a lung. He struggled to move, and instead of pushing against membranes so tight it was useless, he flew up with his effort and fell right off the bed, landing on where his nose should have been. But instead of a nose, he felt a flatness, and instead of a throbbing pain from falling, he felt as if he had landed face-first on a cushion.

He moved his arms forward to push himself up, and they came easily. He pressed what should have been his hands against the floor. They were nubs without fingers, but when he pushed with them, they held his weight. He rolled back on his now-kneeless legs, until he was sitting upright, legs folded under him like rubber tubes.

He rolled curiously back and forth, but there was no pain at all, only a slight rubbing sensation. No pain at all!

He looked down at himself. His vision was clear now. Clearer than it had ever been. He had grown used to things being a little blurry. They had blurred a little more each year since he was too young to remember. But now, even in the dim light, he could see with perfect sharpness. It seemed much lighter in the room now. He saw shadows where he had never seen them before. Edges where there had been only shapes.

He saw his own arms, pink like the creature's, covered in the yellowed membrane. But the membrane no longer held him. It moved and stretched, just like his skin had. He lifted his arms and made a circle with them. They were easy to lift and did just as he asked.

Evan sprang up, pushing easily off his new nub legs, his heart starting to sing. He could move again! He could see! His legs held him with no trouble. He kicked one out in front of him and then the other. They moved so well!

He could still hear his mother's now-quieter crying from

behind the door. What should he do? Should he call out to her, tell her he would be all right, that he was better now? Or should he leave her, not let her see him? Would seeing him frighten her more than his death?

"Mom!" he said finally, pressing his face against the door.

"Evan?"

He heard her standing, swallowing a last faint sniff. Evan was aware that his voice sounded different, more rough, and lower. He wondered if he would sometimes growl and sometimes hiss, just like the others.

"Yes, it's me! Please don't come in. It will be too horrible, I know it will. It was for me when I first saw one." He heard the doorknob turn, just a little, as though she couldn't think of what to do.

"Mom, I look awful. You'll be disgusted. But I'm all right. I can move again! I'm up out of bed." He heard her sob at this, but with relief.

"Oh, honey," she sobbed. "I don't care how you look. Of course I don't care. You're still my baby, no matter what you look like!"

Evan pushed his body against the door with all his strength. He was much stronger than he had been an hour ago, but he was not sure how strong.

"I care!" he cried. "I care!"

"Oh, honey, you can really move?" She sounded happy. And Evan was happy too. To be walking around and out of bed, no matter what he looked like.

"Mom, I have to go away for a while. I have to go with

them." As he said it, he heard the doorknob from the bathroom turning. Instinctively, fear rose inside him. He tried to keep it out of his voice. "I have to go away because I made a promise. And I have to learn how to live like this. I don't think I can survive here."

He heard her crying softly.

"Baby, just promise you'll come back!" she cried.

"I will, Mom. I'll come visit if I can. But I don't know when that will be. It might be weeks, or years. You can't wait around and worry about me."

He heard the hissing of the worm's nubs sliding across the floorboards toward him. It was much louder than it had been before. He turned slightly to look at it.

It was grinning, its fangs showing deep inside its wrinkled hole.

Evan pressed his new lips together, felt the wrinkled top rub across the wrinkled bottom. The unnatural roundness of them, like a smiley face looking surprised. And inside, deep inside, he could feel his strangely thin tongue press into his own fangs. He looked into the creature's lidless, pale eyes.

"I love you, Mom. It's just goodbye for now." Evan turned all the way around and looked at the thing. "Okay!" he said to it. Why did it have to sneak up on him, crowd him, rush him from saying goodbye?

But as soon as he let go of the door, it opened, and his mother was standing there, her hair totally falling out of her bun now, covered in tears, staring down at the two hideous creatures.

She screamed.

The thing grabbed Evan's body with both arms and started pulling.

"Mom, it's me!" Evan cried. "Don't be afraid!"

His mother rushed forward and threw her arms around him. Evan put his nubs around her as far as they would go. He came up only to her waist now.

The creature tugged, ripping him backward, out of his mother's arms.

She fell forward onto her hands, struggled to push herself up.

"Mom!" Evan tried to wrench himself free, but the creature was too strong. He was hurtling away from her, nubs just off the ground, helpless. *"Mom!"*

The creature's nubs scraped against the wood. The air whooshed by Evan's ears. The thing jerked Evan toward the bathroom. It pushed Evan inside. Then it dropped him, and before Evan could do anything, it slammed the door behind him with a bang.

The creature reached up and enveloped the doorknob with the end of its handless arm, turning the lock. "You must leave her behind now," it rasped.

"I can hear her crying." It was too loud. He wanted to cry too, but his eyes were as dry as paper. He didn't seem to have any tears.

"Don't worry, proem," said the thing. "You will forget."

"I won't—"

"You have tried our patience, new one," it interrupted. Its voice was even stranger, even more cold. It pushed up close to him, its sunken white eyes exactly on his level now.

"What do you mean?" asked Evan, looking around him. Was there any other way out? It was just a normal bathroom, with one tiny window, now boarded up. He'd never known how the worm got in—he hadn't wanted to know.

His mother was still crying. She was trying to turn the doorknob. How could he make it stop?

"One child. In a whole long day."

A chill like drops of ice water ran down Evan's back. "It was all I could do," he stammered, knowing it wasn't. Knowing he had quit, and they must know it.

His mother banged on the door. "Evan! Evan!"

"You have disappointed us," it said, almost a growl now. "We are your family. Your protection." Its arm rested on Evan's back. He felt a strange, rough coldness when the membranes touched.

"I did what you asked and I'm not doing what they asked," Evan growled back, pressing forward, away from its nasty arm. "That should be enough for you." He moved to the side, tried to squeeze around it, but it pushed him backward, toward the bathtub.

Its mouth pressed all together from all sides, into one tiny little point.

"How do you plan to get out of here?" Evan blurted, unable to contain the question.

"We go down the drain," it said. It had pushed Evan all the way against the tub now.

"Evan!" cried his mother. She threw herself against the door. *Bang. Bang.* She was never going to give up. She loved him more than anyone else in the world. Maybe she was the only person who loved him.

But Evan couldn't forget Foul's threat. He had to go, or *they were going to eat her!* How could he protect her if he didn't go? Whatever was waiting for him, it couldn't be worse than what would happen if he didn't. "Down the drain?" he asked. It came out as a whisper.

"You are not a human anymore," it growled, bringing its nub down on the bathtub edge. "Stop thinking like they think." It thrust one of its legs behind Evan's and kicked upward, knocking Evan backward into the tub.

Evan folded up over his middle, but it didn't hurt at all. It was like his insides were made of jelly now. He pushed against the tub, tried to get himself upright, but slipped and fell into a ball.

His mother was cranking the knob again. Now her voice was softer, but she was still saying his name.

"You first, new one." The worm's mouth opened again into a grin, and its nub reached out, pointing to the drain. "I am not leaving you here."

"Stop calling me 'new one'," Evan whispered. He didn't want his mom to hear this. "My name's Evan. My mom knows my name. She cares about me and you don't." *I'm so sorry, Mom,* he thought. *I have to go.*

The creature closed its mouth again. It let out a long wheezing noise that seemed to come from all its pores. "*My* name is

Olen," it said. "You will get a name too, once you come home. Once the others know you can be trusted. You will not be a new one." It sighed again. "But we don't go by our human names. You must forget it."

Evan gaped. He was sure his brand-new fangs were showing. It was the first time the creature had admitted that it had once been human. All this time, Evan had wondered if it was really true, if they had all been human at some point, just like him.

"Yes, we are like you. And you are like us," it said.

The creature was still ugly. It—he?—was still cold and creepy and wished him ill. But now he had a name. Now Evan knew this thing had once been like him, although maybe very long ago. He started to calm down a little, to stare at the drain in the bathtub. The stopper was already out. Olen must have moved it when he'd come up. It was so small.

"What do I do?" he whispered. "Mom, I'm okay! I'll come back, I promise!" he called to her.

"I love you," she answered. She had stopped cranking the knob. He could hear her labored breathing, the quiet tap of her hand as she pressed it against the door.

"I love you, too," he called.

Olen's wrinkled hole-for-a-mouth pinched. "You put your legs together, and then you put your arms against your body," he said, his voice edged with malice again. As he demonstrated, he seemed to melt all together into one tube, like he really was a giant worm. "Then you slide over the hole and travel down." He shook a little, and his arms and legs popped out again.

"Where do I come out?" Evan asked. He thought it was a reasonable question, but the worm's face wrinkled in anger.

"Enough questions! We should have been back home already!" Olen clambered over the side of the tub and wrapped an arm around Evan's, pulling him up. "Can't you grip the tub, new one? Did you get Higger slime for membrane?"

"What?" Evan felt the bottom of the tub with his leg stumps. His legs grated against the surface. They *were* gripping it somehow. He took a step, then another, until he was standing just above the drain, one nub on either side. He turned himself around to face Olen.

Olen nodded. Though he had no chin, his body bent a few inches below his mouth.

Evan laid his arms against his body, felt them sink into his side. He clamped his legs together, and they stuck and melded. He wanted to cry out, scared of being immobile again, but he choked it back. He tried to close his eyes, but he had no lids. They stayed open, staring at Olen's ugly face. He slid backward and let himself begin to fall.

THIRTEEN

INSTINCTIVELY, HE PRESSED his now-soft body against the sides of the pipes, twisting and turning so he would slide. Down through the house and under the ground, he felt his location compared with the surface as he had once felt his feet when compared with his face.

He slowed as the pipe leveled under the surface and dropped him out into a larger pipe, legs first. His body expanded quickly, but with no pain. He slid into the sewage, aware that he should be screaming, disgusted, madly wiping the stuff off. But he realized he couldn't smell it. Did he have any sense of smell at all? He rolled up until he was standing, never thinking about what to do or how to do it. He was able to stand up straight. The top of the pipe was nearly a foot above his new, short head.

Olen dropped out of the pipe a second later, landing squarely on his legs. He looked at Evan and smiled.

"Rough landing, new one?" he chortled.

"You smell like you've had a few," said Evan. "And why can't I smell anything now?"

"You hear very well, don't you?" Olen asked. He slid by Evan and along the bottom of the pipe, oblivious to the liquid goop that rose up nearly to his middle.

Evan couldn't argue with that, and he wouldn't miss the

smells down here. He shuffled after Olen, amazed at how easily he moved. The liquid seemed to fall off of him without making him wet. As they went he checked his bearings, trying to figure out what direction they were going in.

Olen must have seen him looking back. "Hoping to find your way home again?" he said with a mean laugh.

"Why shouldn't I?" Evan answered, figuring there was no point in denying it. "My mother has seen me already, and I promised her I'd come back. There's no law against it, is there?" Evan stared back at where they had come from. They had just rounded a corner, and there were smaller pipes on either side just after it, each dropping a small waterfall of greenish liquid into the stream they were walking through. There had been no major forks, but still Evan felt hopelessly lost. The sewer was so strange and foreign.

"No law against it. We don't have laws," said Olen. "But you will not want to go up there if you can help it."

Evan turned back to look at him. Their sunken white eyes met. Olen's glowed a little.

"Was it hard for you to come up and see me?" Evan asked. It was the first time it had occurred to him that tormenting him might have been a chore for Olen.

"I did it for the clan," he said. His voice was more growly than ever. "You are part of the clan now. You are a Wuftoom. Now you will hate being aboveground as much as I do."

I love being aboveground, he thought. *I love my mother.* But he said nothing.

Olen turned and slid on, sloshing more than before.

For the first time, Evan realized that it was dark down here, so dark that as a human he would have stumbled and moved slowly, grasping at the walls. As it was, he saw the passage clearly, although the tint of everything was slightly green. Without thinking, he rushed after Olen, the liquid still sliding off him harmlessly.

Evan wondered if he could ever like being like this. At that moment he hoped he would. Life would be so much better if he could only like it and not want to go back. "So you like it now? Being a worm?" he asked.

Olen whirled around on him, churning the water. "I am *not* a *worm!*" he growled. Evan stepped backward, but Olen closed in. "We are Wuftoom! We are the strongest in the dark places. We are the smartest and the longest lived. Long after the rest have been destroyed and the trees have withered into ashes, we will still be here."

Evan shrank back farther in the face of Olen's wide-open mouth and sharp, pitiless fangs. "What about the bugs?" he stammered.

"They are numerous," Olen spat. The spittle hit Evan's cheek and slid down, but it rolled off him like the water.

"It said they eat you . . . us," Evan said. "Do they get many?"

Olen pursed his shriveled lips. "No. They aspire to eat us. We are a delicacy among dark creatures." He gave a humorless chuckle. "But they do not get us."

"It said that they want to destroy you. That you want to destroy them."

Olen examined Evan. Evan could feel the thing's eyes on

him like lasers. The stare lasted an eternity. Suddenly, Olen sat down in the mucky stream. Since he had no proper waist or joints, he simply bent in two, his legs sticking out in front of him, pressed together underwater.

"You are one of us now. You need to know," he said.

Slowly, Evan sat down in front of Olen. They sat in the middle of the stream, now covered up to the tops of their arms. Yet Olen did not appear to notice the flow of sewage rolling over his body.

Although Evan could not smell it, he could imagine its smell. As he remembered Olen's stink, it seemed to waft into his brain. *Stop,* he thought. *It isn't there. This is natural for me. Just like it used to be natural to take a bath.* He tried to breathe calmly as the muck flowed over his body.

"Wuftoom are ancient. We have lived since the earliest men came to this place. No one knows how the first one appeared. But we spread through the greed of men. In killing and eating the first one, they made more of our kind. Until they stopped eating us, and we had to find another way. Now we bury our dead in the open and wait."

"But why do you do it in a field? Why not in the middle of the town where everyone would step in it?" Evan asked.

Olen grunted. "We only wish to replace those who have died. We could not feed any more," he said, pursing his shriveled lips again. "The bugs—they are called Vitflys—grow more numerous each day. Their insatiable appetites belie their diminutive size."

Evan thought that at a foot long, they were hardly diminutive. He had seen their fangs and their glowing yellow eyes. He believed that they could eat a lot. He rubbed his arms together uncomfortably and was again aware of the sewage flowing over him.

"Do you both eat the same things?" he asked.

Olen nodded. "There are those who would make more of us now, the better to destroy them. But if we should do that, the whole clan would weaken and starve. So we must destroy them with what we have. The water and the walls listen, so I can speak no more of that." Olen inclined his head, and Evan looked but saw nothing except slimy walls and slowly drifting sewage.

"You said things would be better," said Evan. "That we were going to leave the sewers."

"I did not lie," said Olen. "Once the Vits are gone, we will have no need to hide here in the water. We will go wherever we please, live how our ancestors intended."

Evan did not ask where that was, or how they were supposed to live. All he could think of were the Vits. "But what are they? Where do they live?" Evan remembered Foul's size, its fangs, the sound of its wings beating. He pictured Foul dropping between them, opening its mouth wide to show its pointed fangs, then sinking them into Olen, covering Olen in yellow-pink worm juice. He tried to blink to wipe away the image but was reminded that he had no eyelids.

"They are a much younger race than we." Olen's mouth twisted with disdain. "They appeared in the last century, much smaller at first, blending in with other flies. About fifty years ago, they suddenly began to grow. Since they have reached their present size, they make no secret of their desire to rid the dark places of us."

Evan wondered if people had seen them. If they had buzzed around his house when his grandmother was young. "You're the oldest, but you're only as old as people?" he asked. "Weren't there lots and lots of animals before people evolved?"

"Men were the first with intelligence," Olen replied. "I'll give them that." This didn't really answer Evan's question, but before Evan figured out what he wanted to ask, Olen was already talking again.

"The Vits live underneath us, mostly. In the deeper holes that weren't made by humans. They think they're better than us for that, but they didn't make them either. They can live anywhere that's dark. Hollow trees, caves, basements."

"Do they come out at night?" Evan asked, thinking of his mother.

"They tolerate it better than we do, but the open air still isn't good for them. Of course, they only eat below."

"Why? Nobody knows about them. They could get away with anything." The thought sent another chill down Evan's spine. He thought about the school and all the kids milling around, with the Vitflys waiting in the basements to come up.

"For the same reason we eat only the dark creatures," said Olen. "It is how we are made. There are two worlds, you see. The world of the humans and what they see, and ours. We are forced to see their world because it is so large and powerful, but we wish we could not. We wish we could be as ignorant as they are."

Evan wished he was still ignorant, just like everybody else. Yet the feel of the sewage rolling over him had become calming, and Olen's face seemed less disgusting now.

"What about the square they gave me? Where did they get it? Can they get into our minds?" This was the thought Evan had been pushing away. The thought he did not want to face.

Olen twisted his lips. Evan could not read the expression. "It was stolen from another creature. An old race that had much knowledge of the mind. They try to mold it to their purpose, but they do not know how to use it."

"But they talked to me in my head," said Evan. "While I was out of my body. Can't they get into me again?"

Olen's mouth twitched into a small smile. "You are a Wuftoom now. Humans have weak minds, but we are strong. The Vits have transmitted a word or two, no more. Their minds cannot beat ours the way yours beat the other boy."

Evan was not comforted. The worm was too smug, and Evan didn't trust his judgment. But Olen seemed to think that was the end of it. He stood up to go.

Evan could do nothing but follow. His head spun with what Olen had said. We must destroy them. Two worlds. The water and the walls listen. He looked around him as he walked. He saw nothing, but the more he thought about it, the more he felt a presence, or more than one. Was it his imagination?

Before long, they reached a place where pipes emptied into the large stream from either side. They emptied at about Evan's head level. Olen went into the left pipe, lifting himself up easily with both arms. He stood up, his head nearly touching the ceiling of the smaller pipe.

Evan looked at him nervously. He didn't know if he had the strength to pull himself up that far.

"We're stronger than we look," said Olen. "Don't think, just move."

Evan set his arms on the bottom of the pipe as he had just watched Olen do. The pipe was slimy, and without fingers, he felt sure his nubs would slip off. How had his legs gripped the bathtub? He slid his arms back and forth and looked up questioningly. His arms felt as weak as jelly.

"Just move," Olen repeated.

Evan squeezed his eyes in imitation of closing them and pushed against his jelly arms. They stiffened and clung to the surface of the pipe. His body rose into the air, and at the same time his arms lengthened, allowing his legs to make it into the pipe without him having to release his arms. Once he was standing in front of Olen, his arms came up from the pipe with a pop of releasing suction and slowly shrank back to their normal length.

Just as Evan turned back to face where he had come from, his powerful hearing picked up a scraping noise. Below him in the main pipe, a giant spider slipped from a hole on the far side. It was the biggest spider Evan had ever seen, even bigger than the tarantulas in the zoo. It would have fit neatly in a soccer ball.

It fell into the water for a second, then jumped onto the wall and crawled away sideways, staying above the water line. It scurried so fast that it was soon tiny in the distance. After it came another and another and another. As soon as they were out of their hole, they stopped going one by one and followed the first one in a pack, filling the whole wall for several feet. The pack scurried with the scraping sound Evan had first heard. It faded quickly as they got farther away.

"Clever bastards," said Olen, almost laughing.

"What are they?" Evan asked, amazed and disgusted. They had moved too fast for him to see well, but they had looked hairy and black.

"They're Dark Spiders. Like your spiders, only larger and intelligent. They talk just like you and me."

Evan gaped in amazement.

Olen smiled. "All of the true dark creatures are intelligent. They talk. Some even read and write."

"And nobody knows about it? Nobody has seen them?"

"Everyone has seen them," Olen said. "In the dark places."

Evan wondered what life would be like if people knew these creatures existed. Would they try to communicate with them, or would they destroy them? Evan wasn't sure, and the thought made him squirm. Maybe the dark creatures were smart to hide. Maybe he would be smart to hide now.

"Do you talk to them a lot?" Evan asked.

"Oh no, we eat them," he laughed. "That's why they waited until we were up here to leave their hole." His laughter was like an earthquake now that Evan heard so well.

"You eat intelligent creatures?"

"You can't eat the stupid ones," Olen scoffed. "Then you'd

be stupid too." He turned and started sliding down the smaller pipe. It was even darker, but Evan could still see perfectly well.

"But that's nonsense!" Evan cried. "People eat all kinds of animals and plants that don't talk. It doesn't make them stupid."

Olen whirled on Evan. "When will you understand?" he growled, poking his arm into Evan's middle. "We are not human! We are not like them at all. You are not an animal. You are a dark creature. You are something entirely different from them. Everything you know about life as a human is wrong now." He poked Evan harder.

"Okay! I get it!" But he didn't get it. He didn't understand how eating something that talked could be okay. That meant the Wuftoom were just as bad as the Vitflys. He wondered if the spiders had a name other than Dark Spiders that they used among themselves. If they would be just as angry to be called spiders as Olen was to be called a worm.

They slid in silence down the pipe. It twisted and turned, and smaller pipes dumped their loads into the bigger pipe in tiny waterfalls. After a long while of walking in silence, they reached another fork.

Then he saw them. More Wuftoom. Evan couldn't tell how many there were, but he thought there were at least six, maybe even more. The one standing at the front of the pipe gave Evan a big smile. His fangs were both wider and longer than Olen's, but he was shorter than the rest. His eyes glowed bright. He jumped lightly down in front of Olen and pushed past him to examine Evan.

"Well, well," he said, his voice low and gravelly, still smiling.

"Our proem is full grown." He circled Evan and examined him from every angle.

Evan was suddenly aware that he was naked, something he had not really noticed since he became a worm. "A fine transition. Fine indeed. Master Olen, this is great work!" He clapped Olen heartily on the back.

Olen smiled, his eyes also glowing white. "New one, meet Master Rayden, our clan head."

Rayden nodded approvingly. "On behalf of us all, I welcome you to the dark!" He smiled broadly, showing his large fangs, and gave Evan the same back clap. It was so hearty that Evan was nearly knocked forward into the water. Olen's mouth twisted, as if he was trying not to laugh.

Evan was confused by the newly lightened mood. The six or more pairs of eyes glowed at him from the pipe beyond. He forced himself to nod.

"Have you frightened this one so much?" said Rayden, turning to Olen. Both Wuftoom grinned large. Rayden turned back to Evan. "I apologize for Master Olen's behavior. He sometimes forgets that proems are not human."

Evan didn't know what to say, so he nodded again.

"Now, please don't take offense to this, though it will not be pleasant. You cannot know the way until you have your name." Rayden waved his arm, and three more of the waiting Wuftoom jumped down into the pipe. One of them carried a dark black cloth. He walked up to Evan without saying anything and tied it around his eyes.

For the first time since becoming a Wuftoom, he was in total darkness. Panic shot through him. It felt terribly, terribly wrong. His body seemed to close around him, and he felt like he wasn't getting any air. He gasped. Then he felt an arm on his shoulder and heard Olen's voice.

"I know this isn't easy, new one," he said. "We aren't meant to be blind. But rest assured, we will take care of you."

That was the nicest thing Evan had ever heard Olen say, but he was too frightened to be grateful. Without thinking about it, he raised his arms and struck out in all directions. He felt cold arms wrap around his arms tightly, and then his legs, and he was being hoisted up and carried.

As they went, Evan calmed down a little, but just a little. He had been blindfolded as a human before. He had been in rooms so dark he couldn't see. But this was nothing like that. This was like hanging from a windowsill by two fingers, with nothing below you but thirty floors of air.

Instead of his heart beating fast and his lungs pumping, the fear was in his whole body. He tried to breathe deeply, but no air came in. He heard a few voices, as if from very far away. Someone asked Olen how the trip had gone, and Olen gave some reply. Someone said something about proems, but Evan was too distracted to understand.

The journey seemed to go on for hours, even though deep inside Evan knew it probably was not that long. They twisted and turned. He was lifted from arm to arm, up sometimes and down at others. The Wuftoom squooshed him and pulled him and sucked him through pipes and carried him again. Suddenly, a heavy stream of water drenched him from above, and then several arms set him down on his legs. Someone removed the blindfold.

Evan's whole body gasped for air, so that at first he still couldn't see where he was. But, slowly, his vision cleared. He was staring at a concrete cave. In the cave were a hundred Wuftoom, all staring at Evan, their white eyes glowing in the dark.

FOURTEEN

A FEW SECONDS WENT BY in silence, with Evan staring at the Wuftoom and the Wuftoom staring back at him. A low growl spread through the room, growing until it filled the cave. Then the creatures were surrounding him, clapping him on the back with their nub arms, smiling at him and showing their fangs of different lengths.

"Enough!" called Rayden, who was standing behind Evan. Though all the Wuftoom looked almost exactly alike, Evan was starting to see what might differentiate one from another. Rayden was both shorter and broader. His large fangs were coupled with thick arms. The membranes were tight around his body, while some of the others' membranes were loose and hung off them like they were a few sizes too big.

Evan's own membranes were somewhere in between. Slightly loose, but not quite saggy. The baggy ones gave the impression of age.

"This is a great day for the Wuftoom! We shall welcome the new one as befits our splendid race!" cried Rayden.

Another growl came up from the crowd, this one louder than the first. Without apparent direction from anyone, the Wuftoom cleared out the center of the cave. From the back of the cave, several of the creatures brought out a bunch of plastic-looking rods and began putting them together. Soon Evan could see that they were making a simple scaffolding tower. A large clear bowl, which also looked like plastic, was placed on top.

After clearing the other workers away, one of them jumped into the air and caught himself on one of the rungs of the structure, so that he was hanging from his fangs. He let out a room-shaking growl and jumped down, landing in a hole just big enough for him. As he squeezed back into the crowd, flames rushed up into the air until they were searing the bowl.

"Did he just light a fire with his fangs?" Evan whispered to Olen.

"It's a skill that takes much practice," said Olen. "But you will master it in time."

Evan stared as the flames rose and licked the bowl. It was not opaque but not quite clear. Not like any plastic he'd ever seen. "What's it made of?" he asked.

"Membrane," said Olen. "It keeps away both the water and the heat."

"You mean that's someone's skin?"

Rayden laughed, a deep, strong sound. "Put those human sensibilities aside, new one. The former owner of that membrane had a good, long life. There's probably something of him in you now." Rayden laughed harder at seeing Evan's face.

Evan knew he was talking about the pit full of dead Wuftoom that Evan had stepped in. "Is that what happens to everyone?" he asked finally, thinking about how people buried their dead in graves, or scattered their ashes in their favorite places.

"So far," said Rayden, still jolly.

Evan looked up at the structure, which though full of fire did not seem to be burning. "Is it all coated with membrane?"

"Olen, I think we've got a smart one," Rayden replied.

The fire burned higher. Evan was about to ask what they were going to do with it when the crowd made way for three Wuftoom, each carrying a mass of something hairy in his arms. When Evan saw a leg stick out, he recognized the spiders they had seen earlier scurrying frantically away.

Each of the three Wuftoom appeared to be carrying at least ten spiders. Oohs and ahs and wordless growls came from the crowd. The cries only got louder when the three Wuftoom started throwing the spiders one by one into the bowl, completely whole. They fried and popped.

The other Wuftoom began to sit down in the water, which flowed nearly up to their shoulders when they were sitting. There was much laughter and shouting. Evan saw them stick their noses into the sewage and drink from it, and he nearly gagged.

Olen looked at him for a few seconds. Then Olen and Rayden each grabbed a side of him and pushed him down, so that he was underwater. It happened so fast, he didn't have a chance to close his mouth. Quickly, they pulled him back up again. Both were grinning at him. To his surprise, the water had felt cold and clear, like drinking from a mountain stream. Evan stared at them.

"Sorry, new one," said Rayden, clapping him on the back again. "It's the only way to get used to it. Now let's eat!" Rayden pushed through the group of creatures toward the fire, and Evan followed with Olen behind him. There was a space at the front that had been left clear, just the size of three Wuftoom. Rayden sat down and motioned for Evan and Olen to do the same.

Olen sat, leaving a space between himself and Rayden.

Having no other choice, Evan squeezed himself between them. Their membranes were cold against his own. The sewage flowed over him and felt calming and clean.

He wished he could close his eyes so he could feel it all and figure it all out. He was conscious of the Wuftoom staring at him. The several worms who sat with them eyed Evan openly.

"We will eat," said Rayden to Evan, "and then we will introduce you to the young ones. You will stay with them, and they will help you to adjust."

"Is Olen one of them?" Evan asked.

Rayden looked at Olen and they both laughed. "Master Olen is one of the oldest," said Rayden. "He's been a Wuftoom since before the white men settled the northwest."

"You must be two hundred years old!"

"That must seem very old to a new one," said Rayden. "But it is not so old to us. I am more than two hundred years old myself."

Evan stared at Rayden, then at Olen. Evan had no idea what to look for as signs of age. Like Evan's, Olen's membranes were neither tight nor loose. Evan had thought Rayden was younger because of his tight membranes and thick arms. They all had the same shriveled lips and smooth submembrane skin.

Suddenly, the crackling sounds increased wildly. The spiders were so hot, they danced in the fire. Evan was sure the black smoke rising from the bowl should have smelled foul, but he smelled nothing. There was a restlessness around him that meant only one thing: hunger. They were so close to the fire that the water around Evan began to feel warm, even through his membranes. It was like taking a pleasant bath, only one that awakened him instead of putting him to sleep.

Wuftoom approached the fire and reached up with long rods to pull the spiders out. At the same time other Wuftoom tossed fresh spiders on the fire.

Someone dropped the first spider into Rayden's arms. It would have burned a human's skin, but Rayden appeared not to notice. His membranes clouded slightly as the spider steamed. Next, the Wuftoom gave one to Evan. Instinctively, Evan nearly dropped it for fear of the heat, but he found that it was only pleasantly warm, and his membranes also took on a cloudy shade.

As the Wuftoom passed the spiders out, Evan thought about how he had watched them run. Was this one of the same ones? And Olen had said they talked, that they were intelligent just like Wuftoom.

As they passed beyond the elite group, the servers no longer gave whole spiders but began splitting them in half. At first nobody ate, and the agitation in the cave rose. Evan himself was salivating, trying not to think about the spiders talking, then salivating more. Everyone seemed to be waiting for something. Then Rayden stood up and raised his spider, giving a loud, wordless grunt. The spider's legs stuck out from its fat and meaty body. The sight of it made Evan ravenous.

Crunches came from all around him as the Wuftoom fed. Evan hesitated, but soon he could take it no longer. He bit into the creature's leg. For the first time he realized he had more teeth than just the fangs. They were so small and inlaid that they couldn't be seen from the outside, but Evan felt them cutting into the thing's flesh.

He had never tasted anything like it. It was meaty and salty and sweet at the same time. He took another bite and another. An unknown liquid seeped out of the thing and dripped down his chest, but he didn't care. Before long, he had eaten the whole thing and hurriedly wiped his mouth, looking up to see if there was any more.

Rayden was looking down at him with an amused twist to his shriveled hole. The same green liquid dripped down beneath his mouth. A few dark hairs stuck to his cheek.

"Like it?" he asked.

Evan said nothing, suddenly embarrassed. Had the other Wuftoom eaten with such gusto? Across the room, some were just getting fed from the second batch of spiders. With relief, Evan watched them tear into theirs. But then he realized that these Wuftoom were tearing into half spiders. A whole one had done nothing but make him hungry! How could they take it?

Rayden wiped his face with his arm, then pressed his wrinkled lips to the same arm and sucked. His mouth moved back and forth across the arm until he had sucked up all of the green juice. Evan turned and saw Olen doing the same thing.

A few in the back were still eating, but all the worms had torn through their spiders at amazing speed, and most were either finished or just licking their arms. Rayden stood up and faced the circle. Many growled for more. Others just growled.

"A story!" Rayden cried, raising both arms. "For the new one!"

"For the new one!" a chorus echoed. It was so loud it made Evan's flesh shake, but it felt friendly. There was a loud slurping noise as the Wuftoom, now finished with their meal, bent down toward the sewage and drank, almost in unison. Evan followed their lead and felt the freshness drip down his throat.

Rayden stood up and stepped forward, turning to face the crowd. He smiled, showing his extraordinary fangs, and raised his arms. "This is a great day!" he cried. His deep, gravelly voice boomed through the room. "We finally have a new one among us!"

A shout of agreement rose up from the crowd.

"This is the beginning of a great era for Wuftoom!"

Another shout.

"An era in which we shall grow, and grow stronger!"

"A thousand more!" someone cried. A chorus agreed.

"Now, now," said Rayden with a big, fang-baring smile. "First things first!"

Laughter and shouts of "Destroy the Vits!" "Eat them!"

"For now, a story!"

Shouts.

"Tonight, an old one, from near the beginning. I was not there, but I heard it from someone who heard it from someone who was!"

Laughter.

"It begins in a graveyard."

"Grrr!" the crowd growled.

"Now, in those days, the Wuftoom had plenty to eat. They were the rulers of the dark!"

"Still are!" someone shouted. The crowd roared its agreement.

"And the humans were scarce. They did not have the cleverness to threaten us."

"Still don't!" someone else shouted. Even Evan laughed at that.

"The humans lived in small villages," Rayden continued with a fanged grin, "and moved according to the seasons. They hunted their creatures and ate them, thinking nothing of expanding, but only desperate to survive the best they could.

"They had not invented these fine contraptions they called the sewers, so we lived in caves and tunnels we dug out ourselves!"

The crowd roared in approval.

"That's right, brothers, we did without the humans, except for one thing!"

Boos.

"That's right, we still did need them!" Rayden shrugged and

gave an "oh well" look. "They were scarce, but we were even scarcer! There was unrest. Yes, brothers, there was discontent among the youth."

The crowd laughed.

"Discontent among many who wished the Wuftoom would grow stronger."

A group sitting together near the back wall roared.

"A young Wuftoom had a plan to make it happen. The elders were wary, but they, too, feared eventual decline. A disease was killing off the Wuftoom. One by one, year by year, while very few were being made. There was an air of desperation.

"When the humans returned to Wuftoom territory, fresh from the summer, numerous and healthy, the plan was put in motion. The dead from many seasons were retrieved from their eternal rest. They were stored in membrane, and when night fell, the young Wuftoom braved the surface. They laid the remains next to where the humans slept and waited for the morning. The air had burned their skins and they had risked exposure, but their purpose was accomplished! For when the men arose, they stepped through the dead and were infected."

Shouts of "Yeah!" and "Grrr!" roared through the crowd.

"Nearly all the human tribe fell ill. The Wuftoom watched eagerly and waited, while the humans prayed and performed dances for the spirits. Then one day they finally transformed."

A cry of horror from the crowd.

"Yes, in the daytime! The proems had sheltered themselves the best they could, but humans lived in the air then, not inside as they do now. The proems screamed, and the unaffected screamed louder. The few remaining humans began to slaughter the new Wuftoom, terrified of what they did not understand. The Wuftoom rushed in!"

More cries of horror.

"Yes, in the daylight! The Wuftoom rushed in to save their kin! Their skins burned and their flesh melted inside! Those humans who had murdered proems were covered in the remains of their loved ones—infected. The Wuftoom herded off their survivors, both new ones and old ones screaming with the same cries! When they had returned underground and nursed their wounds, they found that half the original clan had been lost, either to the humans or to the sun. And many of the old ones were melted beyond recognition, still living, but crippled so that they could no longer maintain their shape. Blind!"

The crowd gasped, and the ones in the back booed. They obviously didn't like the story anymore.

"But the clan was increased overall." Rayden nodded to the hecklers with a grin. "And even more so, when all of the remaining humans were transformed. The village became an empty shell. The Wuftoom salvaged what could be used, and the rest blew away on the night wind. The blind and melted became heroes, and the tragedy became a song."

The hecklers roared and splashed sewage among themselves.

Rayden smiled and shook his head. "But the years went by. Summer after summer, and no humans came. The demise of the entire tribe had caused the humans to believe the valley cursed. Now, the network of tunnels the Wuftoom had built, it was not as extensive as the sewers. It did not connect with those of other creatures, for there were no others capable enough to build them. The Wuftoom faced a choice. Wait for the humans and slowly die, or move to where the humans were.

"So they started digging, and it was a hard life. Many were worked to their deaths, others burned by the night air while keeping the rest safe. The group that reached a village were few and battered." Rayden paused and the crowd was silent.

"A few of the young ones suggested they needed numbers fast. They suggested the Wuftoom retrieve their dead, then sneak into the village at night and set a trap." Rayden stared down at the crowd, turning first to Evan's right, then to the center, where the leader's eyes rested on Evan himself. Finally, Rayden turned to the hecklers, who were whispering discontentedly among themselves. "The cycle of disaster began again. The young ones had not learned from the old ones' mistakes."

One heckler stood up and raised his arms. "No one suggests we take them all!" he bellowed. "There are so many humans, we couldn't do it if we tried! We only need more to fight the Vitflys!" His friends howled their agreement.

"It is only a story," said Rayden. He said it calmly, but his voice carried as well as the heckler's. "Take it as you will." And he stepped out from the center and worked his way into the crowd, who were now beginning to stand. Some clapped him on the back as he went by; others shouted friendly greetings. It was clear Rayden was not only their leader but also a well-regarded Wuftoom.

Evan thought about the story. He knew what Rayden was

trying to say. That the Wuftoom should be cautious about taking too many humans. But the heckler's voice stuck in his head. *We need more to fight the Vitflys.* Were the Wuftoom in danger of losing? Which side should he be on? Evan didn't have time to think about it long, because Rayden was soon back at his side.

"Well, new one, what did you think?" he asked in his deep voice, his nub arm on Evan's back.

"It was interesting, Master Rayden," said Evan. "Did that really happen?"

"Oh, Master Rayden only tells true stories," said Olen. He had not said a word since the beginning of the story, but he had watched Rayden with an approving expression.

Rayden showed his large, thick fangs, with what Evan hoped was a friendly smile. "Oh, yes, that one is quite well known. Sometimes the young ones just need reminding. Now, let me introduce you to them. Of course, they aren't as young as they used to be — the youngest has been one of us for seven years."

FIFTEEN

NODDING GOODBYE TO OLEN, Rayden steered Evan away from the center group and to the left. Evan realized they were nearing the group that had heckled Rayden. They were now sitting close together in a circle, in heated debate.

"Ah, the young ones!" Rayden exclaimed, smiling his broad smile. The group paused in their debate to regard Rayden as he addressed them.

"This is the new one. He has yet to earn his name, so you can call him whatever you'd like. New one, meet the young ones. They will take care of you." Rayden's voice was still jovial in its roughness, and he gave Evan another hearty back clap.

The young ones stared at him in silence, and Evan was conscious that others were looking his way as well. Finally, one of them spoke.

"We'll take good care of him," he said, nodding at Rayden. Evan realized it was the one who had stood up and challenged the older Wuftoom.

"That's what I need to hear!" bellowed Rayden, and he clapped the heckler heartily before sloshing back into the crowd. There was another long silence. Their white eyes stared.

"Hello," said Evan.

"The first new one in seven years!" cried the heckler. "I'm

Tret, and these are your new friends." He waved to the group of seven others who surrounded him. They all smiled with their fangs showing and growled a welcome.

"We all know how hard it is to be a new one," said Tret seriously. "We want you to feel like this is your home." Tret put his nub arm around Evan and squeezed.

Tret's group were still smiling at him. When Olen had smiled like that, Evan the human boy had cringed in terror. But their smiles suddenly made him feel safe. He felt the water, which was nearly past his legs in this part of the cave. He didn't know if it was pleasant or disgusting anymore. He wanted to shower himself in it and run away at the same time. His confusion must have shown on his worm face.

"Don't know whether to run or cry, eh?" said Tret. "Well, we've all been there. Why don't you sit down and have some dessert with us."

The whole group sat down again, and the water came nearly up to Evan's mouth. Evan wondered what these creatures could possibly consider dessert. He turned to look and saw a few Wuftoom working their way through the crowd, carrying membrane scraps like trays. On top of the trays were little balls of something. A cry of excitement went through the crowd around him.

"Mifties! Oh boy, you're in for a treat tonight!" said Tret, clapping Evan on the back and causing the water to spray up and drench his head. It felt cool and pleasant.

"What are they?" Evan asked.

Just as he said it, one of the servers came close enough for him to get a better view. The little balls were actually some kind of creature. They looked a lot like mice, but as the server plopped one into Evan's arms, he saw that it was different.

It had scruffy gray fur like a mouse and was about the same size, but its feet had large green claws that stuck out half an inch beyond the paws. Its dead eyes were also green, staring up at Evan with a knowing glow. *It must be my imagination,* he thought. *It can't be glowing if it's dead.* Yet it seemed to. Evan felt sure that a creature like this would be able to talk too, just like the Vitflys and the spiders. The thing's belly was strangely bare. It looked almost like human skin.\

"Just try it," said Tret happily, eyes glowing. He bit his in two and chewed slowly, savoring the taste.

Evan stared back into the green eyes. They seemed to reproach him. Still, everyone else was eating. Evan slowly bit into his. He felt the blood seep over his tongue. It was totally different from the spider. It was dense, dark meat. The blood was thick and bitter. Evan had never tasted anything like it, but Tret was right: it was wonderful. He slurped eagerly at the severed body, sucking the blood in, and finally ate the rest of the mouse thing with one swoop, crunching the sour bones. As he swallowed, a final blast of pleasure floated down his throat.

"Looks like we're lucky to have you with us," said Tret. "There weren't enough to go around."

Evan looked behind him and saw that the Wuftoom on the other side of the room were getting something different, a larger creature with less fur. He heard voices in tones that suggested loud complaining.

"But what *are* Mifties?" he asked.

Tret laughed. "They're the most numerous of all dark creatures," he answered, "but also the most sly. So it's a fine treat when we catch a batch like this. Normally it's just Rayden's crowd that gets them."

"Do they talk?"

Tret laughed louder. "Still a little human! They wouldn't be dark creatures unless they talked. All dark creatures are intelligent. Otherwise, they'd just be animals living underground."

Evan knew what came next. The nonsense about having to eat creatures that talked. Only it wasn't nonsense to them, or to the Vitflys. Olen had been so sure that the Wuftoom were safe. But Evan didn't believe it. Not with the image of hairy, hissing Foul in his mind. Thinking of the Wuftoom the same way the Wuftoom thought of Mifties.

"Do the Vitflys ever get us?" Evan asked. At this the group's mood turned decidedly more somber.

"They like to pretend it doesn't happen," said Tret, nodding toward the center, where Rayden and Olen and the other important worms were sitting. "But three have gone in the past year. Three that weren't retired to the trap. They said they were crushed in a cave-in and had the tunnel full of rocks to prove it. But I think the Vitflys caused the cave-in, and trapped them and ate them, leaving nothing but their membrane."

Evan's arms shook. "Why don't they want anyone to know?"

"Because there are *some* Wuftoom who would respond

by making more of us than just replacements. Enough to raise a real army, to help us obliterate the Vits! The old ones elected Rayden. He's gone from Vit eater to old Nob." The others laughed, but the joke was lost on Evan.

"They think if there are too many of us, we'll all die of starvation. That's what Master Olen said," said Evan. Tret smiled broadly at him, and Evan realized what he'd said. "Us."

"That's right, but we won't. We should make more right when it's time to strike. Then we'll all feast on their blood!" There were growls of agreement from the group. "That means soon, new one! We're closer than we've ever been."

It made some sense, but Evan thought of Rayden's story. "But if there were too many proems, the humans would notice them," he said. "I went to the hospital and I stayed there for months. If more people came in, they'd figure it out. And they wouldn't be as dumb as the people in Master Rayden's story. They wouldn't let the dead ones get all over them. They'd handle them with special gloves and isolate them. They could kill us all if they wanted to." Evan hadn't really thought about it before, but now he was sure. If the whole town got sick, they'd figure it out. Even just two boys being sick might trigger something.

"We've thought of that," said Tret. "That's why we have to get them right away, before they've changed. Most proems don't take nearly so long to change as you did. You took so long that everyone wondered if something had gone wrong. But Olen kept telling Rayden that everything was fine, that you were changing slowly but surely, like he did."

Evan processed this. "Like he did?"

"Oh, yes, old Slow Change Olen."

The group laughed.

"It does something to your head." Tret slapped his head with his nub arm, and the group laughed harder. Seeing the look on Evan's face, Tret gave him a hearty clap. "We'll make sure you don't turn out like him!"

Evan would not turn out like Olen. No matter what happened, he would not. But something else bothered him. "I led a boy into the trap yesterday," he said. "How long will it take him?"

"Oh, one or two weeks maybe," said Tret.

"Weeks!" Evan cried. "But it took me more than two years!"

"We know," said Tret. "I don't think we know anyone who's taken as long as you. Maybe you didn't get enough remains."

"I stepped in it up to my thigh," Evan said nervously. "It took me a long time to get out." Everyone was staring at him. A circle of glowing eyes. Evan was suddenly aware that the rest of the cave was still looking at him too. Worms were sneaking glances from every group. Pretending to be deep in conversation, they all watched him out of the corners of their eyes. He wanted to run. But they would catch him. He wouldn't make it five feet. He tried to smile but knew his mouth was merely twisting into a shriveled, misshapen hole.

"Well, I like anyone who's already tricking the Vits as a pro-em," someone said, grinning.

"Evan, meet Suzie," said Tret, gesturing at the one who had just spoken.

Evan looked at him in surprise. A real name!

"We don't get many females," Tret explained. Evan couldn't see anything different about Suzie that would make her female, but he couldn't ask about it right then because the others were also grinning at him.

"Using the Boomtull Birch to walk a human into the trap was brilliant," said Suzie, grinning.

He wanted to cry out, *I didn't! Olen made me! I tried to stop him!* But he just opened his mouth wide, felt the air over his fangs.

"The Vits tried to get a Wuftoom to spy for them," Tret said.

The rest of the group laughed loudly.

"You see," Tret said to Evan, "they don't really understand what they gave you—the Birch. They can't use it themselves. And they don't understand us. No Wuftoom can be disloyal once we've changed. We all forget about our human cares."

Evan didn't want to forget. He wouldn't let it happen. But he knew he had to pretend his cares were already fading. He had to act like one of them. He tried to smile.

"Isn't Olen crying over the extra mouth to feed?" said the Wuftoom to Tret's left. Everyone laughed.

"This is Ylander," said Tret. "Master Olen's biggest fan."

Ylander grinned and gave a little bow.

"Actually, it was Olen's idea," Tret continued. "Even old Slow Change knows we need to replace the dead. And I have to give it to him, it was a smart plan. We can't rely on people just wandering down there."

"That's what I did," said Evan.

Tret ignored this. "If we could get each one to get one more . . ."

"How are you planning to get a human down here?" Evan interrupted. "Some parts are too small to fit through." He thought about how Jordan would react if he was brought down here before he changed. The creatures. The stink. Evan thought he had hurt Jordan enough already by turning him into a Wuftoom and taking over his last few days as a human. And he was sorry for that.

"We don't need to bring him down here," said Tret. "You see, we've been working on a place to keep them. The old ones aren't happy about it. They see it as the first step toward losing their way on the population question. Which it is. But we tell them we're being extra cautious. You can't be too careful, even if you've only got one proem." Tret showed his fangs.

"Where's this place?" Evan asked. Out of the corner of his eye, he saw Ylander give Tret a hard poke with his nub arm.

"I'm not giving him a map," Tret said, then turned to Evan. "Don't mind him. You're not supposed to know where things are until you get your name. Which doesn't happen until you've proven yourself Wuftoom. We know you're Wuftoom already; it's just an old tradition." This time Evan managed to hold his position under the weight of the back clap.

I am not a worm! he thought.

Just then Evan felt an arm on his shoulder.

It was Rayden. "And how are these fine folks treating you?" he asked, giving a broad grin.

"Really good," said Evan. "Those mice creatures were wonderful."

"Ah, the Mifties! You came on the right day!" Rayden continued on through the cave.

"Even that old Nob will see the logic in it," Tret said. "Once it's done." He leaned his head into the middle of the group. "Ready?" he whispered.

Suzie's mouth opened in a grin.

Ylander nodded.

"You know what to tell Rayden," Tret said to the others.

"What's going on?" asked Evan.

"We'll tell you on the way," said Tret, and he pushed Evan forward, through the group of young ones. The group closed in behind them. In front of them, Evan saw only a drain the size of a shoe box, slowly letting water escape out of the room.

"Just hang on to my arms," said Tret. He jumped into the grate, so that only his head and arms stuck out.

Evan turned to look behind him. Suzie and Ylander were there, grinning. No one else was looking at them. Whatever they were doing, they didn't act like they wanted to hurt him. If he went with them, it could only help him earn their trust. He wrapped his arms around Tret's. Ylander grabbed on to his legs, and before he had time to react further, he was being pulled down.

SIXTEEN

Evan smashed into the water. His whole body gasped, and he splashed himself to standing.

Ylander and Suzie plopped easily into the water behind him. They joined Tret in grinning at him. The membrane on their bald heads rippled.

"What are we doing?" Evan gasped.

"We're going to recover the proem," said Tret. "Come on, we have to get out of here before they notice we're gone and come after us."

"Everyone was looking at me," said Evan, letting the last of the water roll off him.

"All the more reason to move quickly," said Tret, and he wrapped an arm around Evan's back and pushed him forward. "We're supposed to blindfold you, but I think you've been through enough for one night."

Evan stiffened. He felt like his insides were shifting around.

Tret clapped him on the back. "No one's going to do that again. Not if we're with you."

Tret's smile was genuine and his voice was warm. But his face was still Wuftoom. A shriveled hole for a mouth. Sunken white eyes. Evan looked down. As they started moving, Evan's own new face stared blurrily at him from the water. *That is not my face.* He felt himself starting to shake. *Focus on the way,* he thought. He tried to concentrate without showing what he was doing. But he felt sick.

"We've set up in a basement with a big drainpipe," Tret said, "for flooding. The house is abandoned. It's all boarded up. We saw a homeless man there once, but we shooed him off by growling." Tret, Suzie, and Ylander all laughed. "We'll get your friend down there and lock him in until he changes," Tret finished.

"But how are you going to get him down there?"

"That's where you come in, new one! We got the phone working. You'll call him." It sounded so simple.

"I don't know if he'll even remember me," Evan protested. "We weren't friends, and my voice has changed." But he'd done the worst to Jordan already. Being locked in a basement might be better than having to change in front of his parents. His parents wouldn't have to go through what Evan's mom had suffered. Plus, Evan could try to figure out the maze of pipes. "I could try it," said Evan. "I could get him there."

"That's a real Wuftoom talking!" Tret exclaimed, and gave him another hearty clap. Evan was unprepared this time and nearly fell forward onto his face.

As Tret pulled Evan along, he pursed his shriveled lips and whistled. It was a harsh, rasping sound, but then Suzie and Ylander joined in. Somehow, their raspings went together and mixed into a kind of song. It wasn't exactly beautiful, but it wasn't awful, either.

Evan frantically tried to think of what he would say to get

Jordan to the Wuftoom's basement. "I've kidnapped your mother?" "There's buried treasure?" What could he tell him? It *had* to work. He took a glance back. He could see the place where they'd fallen into the big pipe, but he didn't recognize anything else. He wasn't sure if this was even the same pipe that went to the Wuftoom's cave.

They climbed one by one into a smaller pipe. Tret went first, then Evan, then Ylander and Suzie. Something about the smaller pipe calmed Evan. It was just big enough for them to fit through in their full expanded shape, but they had to crawl. He started to feel the water, the way his flexible limbs slid over the metal. The sound of the other Wuftoom breathing filled him. They turned and squished through pipes that got smaller and smaller. As they twisted through forks and squeezed through turns, Evan lost more and more of his bearings, until he despaired of ever remembering the way. And he still didn't know what he'd say to Jordan.

"How do you think he'll react when he sees us?" asked Ylander. "I bet he'll scream!"

"And vomit!" said Suzie.

"He might try to run," said Tret. "We have to be ready for that."

"I didn't do anything," said Evan. Why hadn't he? Why hadn't he thrown something? He could have just turned the light on and Olen would have run.

"Oh, I did!" Suzie laughed. "I barfed all over the place!"

The other two laughed.

Evan managed to fake a grin. *I'm a Wuftoom,* he thought. *It's a joke.* He held the grin until the others had stopped laughing. By that time they had reached a very small pipe, like the one Evan had first gone down.

Evan wondered how on earth he was supposed to go up it. Was he already supposed to know?

"I'll go first," said Tret. "It's important that we go to the right place because it'll be bad enough being aboveground, even if it's good and dark. I'll do the climbing, so you don't have to worry about that now. It's something that takes a little practice. Ylander and Suzie will follow you, so you can't slip back. Now, when I squeeze my head into the pipe, you grab on to my legs."

Evan nodded.

Tret pushed his head, which was nearly as broad as a human head, into the pipe. It squooshed easily without a sound. Evan twisted his nub arms around Tret's sticky, membraned legs. Slowly, they started moving upward. Evan felt Tret's legs glue together as they started entering the pipe, and Evan's arms were glued with them, around each other and around Tret's legs. He felt his membranes rub against Tret's. They were tightly pressed like one big worm.

He felt his head and then his body enter and was surprised to find that his breathing and thinking remained normal. The only way he knew he was all squeezed up was that he couldn't move. The walls of the pipe felt slimy, yet cool and comforting. He felt the stickiness of membrane against his glued-together legs and knew it must be Ylander or Suzie.

They were slowly moving upward, twisting and turning. Evan felt the coolness of the walls and the darkness on his eyes, and the movement was smooth, so that he could almost have fallen asleep, like he was rocking in a ship at sea.

Then his head suddenly expanded to full size. Tret stood above him and reached his arms down. They twisted around Evan's and pulled him out, his body popping outward as he came. Tret pulled Evan onto the floor, where he lay on his back and struggled to breathe. He felt too cold.

With a quiet pop, Suzie and Ylander jumped out of the pipe, landing smoothly on their legs. Evan tried to gasp and his body expanded, but it didn't contract again. He went on expanding. There was too much air inside him. He let out a wheeze.

"Oh, he's never felt the air before!" cried Suzie, rushing over to him. She reached down and curled her arms around Evan's. With her help, he stumbled to his legs, still feeling all wrong.

"What's wrong with me?" he gasped. His voice was harsher and more growly, like he wasn't getting enough air, though he was sure he was getting too much.

"It's the air," said Suzie. "We can stand it if there's no sunlight, but it doesn't feel good. It's like a human holding his breath underwater."

"But I was just up there a few hours ago!" cried Evan. "And I feel like I have too much air, not too little. I feel like I'm going to fly away, break apart, freeze to death." Tret and Ylander were now with him, their lips twisted in the same line.

"A few hours is enough," said Tret. "Once you've been underground, you can't go back." He picked up an old phone from the ground and pulled it over toward him. "We'll make this quick."

Evan sat down in front of the phone, rolling over his rubber legs. It was an old house phone with a cord, so old it had a rotary dial instead of buttons. It was covered in dust.

"Are you sure this works?" he asked.

"Try it," said Tret.

Evan picked it up and put it to the side of his head. He heard a dial tone. "I guess it is working . . . Why are you laughing?"

The three Wuftoom were obviously trying not to smile, and Suzie could barely contain her giggles.

"We don't hear through the sides of our head like humans," said Tret. "We hear through our whole bodies, just like we breathe."

Evan kicked himself. He should have known that. "I know. I just . . ." He tried to smile.

"Take it easy, kid. It's only your first night," said Tret. Evan gasped and stared at the dial. He was getting more and more nervous. What if he couldn't convince Jordan to come down here? He tried to take a breath and was filled with too much air, so much it made him dizzy. He swayed a little.

"We're sorry, new one," said Ylander. "Just hang in there. Make the call and we can go back down."

Evan pulled on the dial, and it spun out of control. Without fingers, his nubs were too big to fit into the holes. He tried to make a point with the flesh of his nub so that it looked like a finger, but it was only a littler nub, all misshapen and still too big. He slammed his nub down on the shut-off. He felt dizzy.

Tret saw his problem. "Look, you have to really concentrate on it. You can make almost any shape, but it won't last long because it takes effort." Tret demonstrated by holding out a nub. A long, thin finger slowly extended from it, then slowly grew back into its normal shape.

But the air was making it hard for Evan to even try. He stared at his nub and willed the point to grow, but only a tiny piece came out. The effort of it made him even more dizzy.

Suzie thrust something at him. It was a metal rod, half the width of a finger and three times as long.

"I found it on the floor," she said.

Evan pressed it between his two nubs as hard as he could. He didn't know Jordan's cell phone number, but he did know the land line. Jordan had used it to call his mother after school. Evan dialed the first number, then the second, then the third, until finally he had dialed all seven. The work of dialing the phone was exhausting. His vision flickered out, then back in. Evan sank to his left and began to fall. Tret caught him.

"Get it together," he whispered.

"Hello?" said a sleepy voice at the other end. It was Jordan.

That snapped Evan back a little. Without thinking, he pressed the receiver to where his ear would be. "Hi, Jordan. It's Evan," said Evan. *Don't ask Evan who,* he thought.

"Evan? Oh . . . hi," said Jordan. Did Jordan know some other Evan? Was it possible that he actually remembered this Evan, to whom he'd barely spoken two words in all their years of school together? At this point, Evan didn't care which.

"Hey, listen, Jordan. I'm sorry I'm calling so late, but what I've got to tell you is really important. I know what's wrong with you. You have the same thing I had."

"How do you know I have something? I don't even know for sure if I have something," said Jordan, his voice tight and on edge.

"I know. It's because I've been through it that I know. People are talking about how you fell into that pit. That's exactly what happened to me."

"You got sick two years ago," said Jordan. "You were in the hospital, and now you're locked up at home dying. That's what everyone says."

Evan had no idea anyone was talking about him. He had assumed they'd never noticed he was gone. No one had ever sent him a card or called. "I'm not dying anymore. But I almost did. The doctors almost killed me. But my grandmother heard about a man who had a cure."

"A man?" Jordan's voice was flat. Evan couldn't tell whether he was buying it or not.

"It's not approved or anything. But I'm better now. You have to come here and get the cure before it's too late."

"You had two years," said Jordan.

"You don't want to go through what I went through!" At least this part Evan could be sincere about. "You don't want to be in the hospital. You don't want to be locked away in a room and have everyone forget about you." Although Jordan's room was quite a bit better than his, he thought bitterly.

There was a pause at the other end. "Where is it?"

Evan stared at a piece of paper Tret had laid in front of him. "Thirteen eighty-seven West Taylor Street. It's a big house that's all boarded up. But the door's unlocked. The door to the basement is in the kitchen. I know it sounds bad, but the guy could get arrested for giving medicine that's not approved. You have to come tonight because he's going away again."

"You really think it's the pit?" asked Jordan.

"The goo," said Evan. "This doctor says it's a parasite. He's tried to tell the other doctors, but no one believes him."

"But I've been feeling bad for a whole week, so maybe that wasn't it."

"It is," said Evan quickly. "And don't tell your parents," he added, trying not to sound like it mattered. "My mom didn't want me to take the medicine. She wouldn't have let me so my grandma had to sneak me out."

"Yeah, you're right," said Jordan. "I'll see you in a little while. Thanks." Jordan hung up, and, slowly, Evan did too, grasping the receiver with both nubs.

"Well?" asked Tret eagerly.

Evan breathed a sigh. This time he felt like he'd gotten the right amount of air. "He's coming," he said. "We just have to wait. But he lives across town from here, so it might take a while." He took another breath. He still felt faint, but he thought he'd be able to hold on.

Suzie was sitting in a ball on the floor. Ylander was standing, but he was leaning against a wall. It looked like they were feeling the effects of the air too. Only Tret seemed to be doing all right. But he saw what was happening to the others.

"Okay, we'll take turns keeping watch for the proem and the rest of us will go back into the pipes. I'll start, and I'll call you after a while," he said to Suzie and Ylander.

They nodded, and without speaking, Ylander went down first. Evan grabbed on to him and Suzie followed. They moved together, snaked around each other, for a short time and then came out in a slightly larger pipe. They were still squooshed down quite a bit and all together like one worm, but Evan still felt better than he had up top. He didn't feel squeezed at all. In fact, he was breathing much better. From the way they were breathing, Evan could tell Suzie and Ylander felt the same.

Maybe it's better this way, he told himself. Jordan wouldn't have to go to the hospital or be locked up in his room. But he also wouldn't have a chance to say goodbye. Evan was glad no one could talk inside the pipe. He wasn't sure he could act the way a Wuftoom should.

SEVENTEEN

JORDAN CAME SOONER than Evan expected. It was still Tret's shift when he pulled the rest of them back into the basement. This time Evan expected the shock, but he still felt the expansion, the cold, the air bursting into his skin. As he struggled to stand, he heard footsteps on the stairs. Suzie and Ylander grabbed him and pulled him into a corner.

"Stay here and flatten yourself," Suzie whispered. Then she, Ylander, and Tret pressed themselves against the walls. They waited by the stairs, ready to jump.

Evan struggled to hold himself. In his mind he knew he was flat, only an inch thick as he spread himself against the wall, but he *felt* like he was growing outward, like he was bigger than ever. He pursed his lips tight.

The room filled with extreme brightness. It was nothing like any light Evan had seen before. It filled the basement, burned his eyes, and wiped his vision into white. He thrust an arm over his eyes, but the light pushed itself in. He tried to keep from screaming and felt a fang press into his tongue. A taste like the spider's filled his mouth.

"Is anyone here?" a voice asked. Jordan.

It was too loud and Evan's body shook. Suddenly, the light was gone.

"What the . . ."

As Evan's vision cleared, he saw two Wuftoom on top of Jordan.

"Okay, let him up, but stay close," said Tret.

Suzie and Ylander climbed off Jordan and lifted him to his feet. He tried to wrench his arms free, but the Wuftoom held him fast. His head turned from side to side, and Evan realized Jordan couldn't see.

"You are Jordan?" asked Tret.

Jordan's eyes focused on Tret's voice. He jerked his arms, and the Wuftoom wrapped their nubs around him tighter. They were much shorter than Jordan, but their worm muscles were stronger than they looked.

"I'm Tret, and these are my friends Suzie and Ylander."

Evan was conscious of how deep Tret's voice was, and how growly. It did not sound human. He had not quite realized how strange it sounded.

"We're not going to hurt you," Tret growled. "We are called Wuftoom."

"Where's Evan?" Jordan asked. He was not shrinking back. He was still pulling against Suzie and Ylander and staring Tret straight in the face, although he could not see him.

"He is here. New one."

Evan popped himself out of the wall and slowly took form. He was still lightheaded, but he was able to stand up. He slowly walked toward Jordan and stood in front of him with Tret.

Jordan must have felt something because he looked vainly around. "Evan? What's going on?"

Evan was speechless. He wanted to say he was sorry, but "new one" the Wuftoom wasn't supposed to be sorry. He was supposed to be glad he'd done this to Jordan.

After a silence Tret spoke. "Jordan, we regret that we were forced to deceive you. There is no cure for what you have. It is not a disease. You will become one of us. We are Wuftoom, the most powerful of races that live in the dark."

Evan couldn't stand it. It was too much like Olen. "There isn't a cure," said Evan. "But we can help you. If you change alone it will be awful. I wish I could cure you!"

"You're not Evan! I bet Evan's dead! What did you do to me? You did it! You took over my life!" It was deafeningly loud. Did the Wuftoom talk quietly compared to humans?

"I am Evan!" Evan said. "I didn't take over your life. I'm trying to help you." He was afraid to tell Jordan the truth.

"You stink," said Jordan. He kicked a foot out and hit Evan in the middle before Tret grabbed Jordan's leg and tugged, sending Jordan, Suzie, and Ylander to the ground. Evan was thrown against the wall. His body flattened, then popped out again. His body expanded too far again, but he wasn't hurt.

His heart sank as he gasped. Kicking the Wuftoom would be worthless. It wouldn't hurt them at all.

"Stop," said Tret quietly to Jordan. "We're trying to help you."

Without being told, Suzie and Ylander picked up some rope from the floor and began tying Jordan's arms and legs. Jordan struggled a little, but he had hit his head badly, and he was no match for the twisting Wuftoom arms that wrapped around him.

Evan tried to keep a blank expression, but inside, his fear was growing. What if he had acted too human? But Tret clapped him on the back silently, as if he'd done well.

Evan knew that tying Jordan up was for Jordan's own good. It would be much worse if Jordan were let loose to change. But these thoughts didn't stop him from feeling sorry for Jordan, from putting himself in Jordan's place and wondering how he would have felt if this was what had happened to him. Evan was stupid enough to have walked into the pit, but Jordan didn't deserve this.

As Tret pulled him toward the pipes, Evan saw Jordan, dazed but awake, twisting his hands in a futile effort to untie the knots. Ylander was standing over him, ready to jump. Jordan screamed, and Ylander clamped a nub around his mouth. Evan could almost feel it, the weight of Ylander's noxious, sewage-dripping body. He felt himself choking as Tret pulled him down into the pipe.

EIGHTEEN

THEY SLID OUT into the larger pipe, but Evan still heard the scream and smelled the stink. He collapsed into the water and covered himself. It made no sense for him to loathe it and bathe in it at once, but Evan felt calmed as the water flowed over him, and his breathing returned.

Tret dived into the water, thrashed around for a few seconds, and jumped back up. He had rolled his belly into a pouch, like he was holding something in it. Evan looked sickly on as Tret let the flap of flesh go and caught a little, scaly, wriggling creature with a rolled-up arm. It wriggled and tried to jump, but Tret held it tight.

"The new one eats first. For a mission well accomplished!" Tret exclaimed. "Now, don't drop it. Eat it quick before it gets away." Tret passed the thing to Evan, who quickly rolled his arm over it and held on tight.

All of a sudden, he felt better. He felt its slimy body wriggle against his skin. It was so strong, it was all he could do not to open his arm up and let it go. Without looking at it, he opened his mouth and pushed the creature in. His fangs and teeth crunched down on its body, which was gooey soft inside. The skin was tough like leather, but it tasted pleasantly sweet.

It stopped moving after his first bite, and he finished it in three quick swallows.

By the time he was done, Tret had risen up with another, which he shared between himself and Suzie.

Suddenly Evan felt guilty. "Are there no more?" he asked.

Tret shrugged. "I don't know. We're lucky we found two. They're getting smarter all the time. The Vits don't go in the water, but since they've been eating the land creatures, we've been taking too many. They know not to travel in groups now."

"What are they?" Evan asked.

"Higgers," Tret said.

"Do they talk?" Evan didn't see how they could.

"They don't talk. They play each other's scales."

Evan thought about this. What would it sound like? "Can you hear it?" he asked.

"No," said Tret, "they only talk to each other underwater. The frogs can hear it, but they don't understand."

"Frogs?"

Suzie giggled. "They're not really frogs. They probably call us worms, like you did." If Evan were still human, he would have turned red with embarrassment, but Suzie didn't seem upset. "They call themselves Orpas, and we call them frogs because they can live underwater for a long time and they hop. They have beady little eyes set way down on their heads and fur that looks like plastic. And their feet have sharp little claws."

"And they just live down here, like you—us?"

"They burrow through the ground and have pools in the

earth where they make their home. They come out here to feed on the tiniest creatures in the water."

"And you eat them, too?"

"Yes."

Evan was silent for a minute. The insides of the Higger had tasted salty and oily. It didn't have as much blood as the spider and the Miftie, but what little it had had melted as it poured down his throat, like warm butter into bread. His mouth watered to think about it again.

"Is there anything you don't eat?" he asked.

"We eat everything that thinks and lives beneath the ground," said Tret.

"We don't eat the Vitflys," said Suzie, "because we can't catch them." She smiled and seemed to be staring at something no one could see.

"Old Rayden ate one," said Tret, staring with the same faraway look.

Suddenly, it was like Evan could read Tret's thoughts. He could taste the phantom of the Vitfly's blood as it trickled, no, poured down Evan's open throat. He could feel the roughness of its wings and the crunch of its exoskeleton against his teeth. His lips pursed together, as if to trap it on his tongue.

Tret noticed Evan's expression and laughed. "You see? All Wuftoom want to eat them. It's Wuftoom nature."

"And they want to eat us . . . Do the Higgers and the Mifties and the spiders want to eat us too?" He didn't know how the Higgers could do it, but what if the spiders had a giant web?

What if they trapped him in it and sucked at him, slurp by slurp?

"Probably." He gave a twisted smile. "Don't worry about the Mitfties." Suzie laughed, but Evan was still worried.

"But what about the Vitflys?"

"They won't catch any more of us," Tret said. He was no longer smiling. He turned his head to directly face Evan, and the water flowed slowly around him as he spoke. "They want to destroy us and have the dark world to themselves. But we will destroy them." His eyes glowed almost as brightly as the Vit's.

"How are we going to do it?" Evan asked. *Please tell me, please,* he thought.

Tret's glowing eyes bore down on Evan as he leaned forward eagerly. He had to lean over Suzie to get his face inches from Evan's. His voice was hissing and soft, but it came through perfectly clear. "We're digging into their home. You see, they think we don't know where they live. They try to make it seem as if they live all over. But they have a home base just like us. It's deep beneath the sewers. They have many tunnels coming out. With false faces and traps to keep it safe from prying eyes. But we know where it is now. We have a weapon that will destroy them!"

At "destroy" he clapped one arm into the other like a man slapping a clenched fist, only when the two arms met, they melted into each other, and Tret's flesh twisted and turned. Suzie grabbed Tret's arms, and they melted their four arms together.

"A weapon?" Evan's heart leaped. "What is it?"

"Shhh!" Suzie whispered. "Someone will hear you. It was another creature who betrayed the Vits to us."

Tret leaned in toward Evan and grinned. A piece of Higger skin hung from one of his yellow fangs. "It's a bomb."

Suzie joined in the grin.

"We've been working on it together," Tret whispered. "We're using our brains from when we were still human. Sneaking into basements at night. Even using their computers. We're finally close to being finished."

"Do the others know?"

"They do now," Tret said. "It's the old scholars who are putting on the final touches. Even old Rayden had to agree once he realized how good it was."

"Who are the scholars?" Evan asked.

"They're a small group of mixed-age Wuftoom," said Tret. "They work on weapons instead of hunting. Rayden's still one of them." Tret turned his grin to Suzie.

She also leaned in close to Evan, so that their three faces were almost touching. "It will destroy them."

"When?" Evan whispered eagerly. If it was soon, he wouldn't have to help the Vits. His mother would be safe.

Tret grinned. "Only a month now."

Evan's heart sank again. He had only three weeks before he was supposed to deliver on his bargain—minus a whole night. If the Vits weren't destroyed by then, he would have to help them. Or they'd eat his mother. He wrapped his own arms and twisted them against his body.

"Why not sooner?" he whispered. He couldn't really look at Tret and Suzie, but stared ahead at the slimy concrete wall.

"We dig every day," Tret said. "We can't go any faster and still have enough Wuftoom to hunt." Tret and Suzie were both smiling, their arms still melting together. They had the same look Olen had when he had told Evan about how wonderful the future would be.

"The other dark places," Evan whispered. Visions of tunnels of earth and stone, caves and streams entered his head. It was far beneath them. He knew it was real and it was down there, waiting. It was instinct for him to know these places and love them, like it was instinct for him to love the creatures' blood.

Did he actually want it? How could he want to live like this? But it was better than what would happen if he helped the Vits. At least the Wuftoom cared about him. Nobody else had ever cared about him except his mother. He wrapped his arms around his legs and melted himself into a ball, letting the water flow over his head. He didn't want to think about his mother.

NINETEEN

THE NEXT SEVERAL NIGHTS were slow. Tret, Suzie, and Ylander took turns watching Jordan while Evan stayed behind with the two who were off duty, sleeping or fishing. They slept during the day, all squished up in the pipes.

During the nights, when they were awake, Evan wished he had a good, long book to slowly work through. Or a movie to watch. Or someone else to talk to. Anything to keep his thoughts off his mother and the Vitflys. But all he could do was think, and the more he thought about it, the less he found any solution. He had to help the Vitflys. But if he did, the Vitflys might win. What would happen to the Wuftoom? What would happen to him?

The only break came when Tret tried to get Jordan to eat a Higger. Evan had pointed out that Jordan might starve before he changed. Of course, Jordan refused to eat it. He spat the Higger all over the floor, where it flopped and shriveled in the air. Tret came down cursing, and Suzie and Ylander laughed and laughed.

"He'll eat when he's really hungry," said Ylander, and sure enough, on Suzie's shift, he took what he was offered.

Suzie laughed as she described the revulsion on Jordan's face.

Inside, Evan cringed. What would it have tasted like, back when he first began to change? Would it have been good like it was now, or barely edible, or worse? He couldn't imagine, and he felt terribly sorry that Jordan was suffering because of him. But he had to laugh with the Wuftoom. He was learning to laugh, to hide his true feelings behind his fangs.

Two nights later Tret finally declared that Evan was ready to take a shift. It was what he had been waiting for. Part of him wanted to hide from Jordan in shame, but a bigger part was desperate to see and talk to him. What had Evan done to him? What would he be like when he changed? Evan also needed to learn to climb. Otherwise, he would never make it back home.

"Can you show me how you go up the pipes?" Evan asked. "I can't hang on to your legs forever."

"We're not allowed to teach you until you have your name," said Tret. "I don't like it, but Rayden would really have my fangs for that."

Evan had to act like it meant nothing, but during the trip he paid close attention to the twists and turns and to the way his membrane hugged the metal.

Jordan was really starting to change, so much that Evan almost cried out in surprise. He was further along than Evan had been only two weeks before he turned. His face was covered in membrane and his hair was patchy. What was left stuck up through the top of his head with unnatural stiffness. His hands curled, and he flexed them compulsively as he watched them approach.

"How are you feeling today?" Tret asked, folding his arms together. By now Evan was able to recognize the real concern in Tret's deep rasp.

Jordan sat still, saying nothing.

Evan's body expanded and contracted, acclimating to the air. He felt dizzy but managed to stay upright.

"Yell if you have any problems," Tret said to Evan. "We'll hear it."

Evan nodded, thankful that Tret was going to leave him alone with Jordan. He hadn't expected that. Did Tret have some idea of what Evan was going through? If so, he made no sign before he disappeared back down the drain. Evan stared at Jordan, who glared malevolently back.

"I just went through it," said Evan. He folded down to the floor. "So I know how hard it is. But it will be over soon. Once you really change, you'll be able to move again, even better than before. And you can see perfectly in the dark. You can't smell the sewage."

Jordan stared at him.

It was obvious that he could see now, and from the hate in his eyes, Evan knew he saw every disgusting feature. He sucked in his shriveled lips, feeling ashamed. He wished he could tell him that he wasn't a worm yet, that he still thought and felt like a human, but he couldn't, so he said nothing else.

Finally, Jordan spoke. "How did you fall into the pit?" he asked.

Evan thought there was no point in lying. "I was skipping

school and I felt like climbing the fence," he answered, "and I just stepped into it." He paused a beat. "How did you fall in?"

Jordan looked at him hard.

Evan's body swelled with the air and he felt colder. He could not let Jordan know the truth. He had to act like he didn't know, or his guilt and shame would overwhelm him.

"I couldn't control my own body. It was like I was possessed. And then one day I walked right into it. I tried to fight, but I couldn't get away. That's what you do, isn't it?" He pulled uselessly against the rope. "You possess people so you can infect them, and then kidnap them so they can't find a cure." He tugged and pulled, but the rope stayed tight in place.

"We don't possess people," Evan said. He tried to keep his voice calm. "And there is no cure. I was in and out of the hospital for months. All the doctors in the world could look for one, but they wouldn't find it. It's not a disease. It's a change. You used to be a boy, but now you'll be a Wuftoom." He paused, then thought of something. "We live a lot longer than people. We live for hundreds of years."

"Hundreds of years?" Jordan screamed. His voice was choked with barely restrained tears. "In the sewers, eating nasty little creatures? For hundreds of years?" Jordan's hands balled up, then flexed again. His body shook as if he were about to sob.

Evan felt stupid. He hadn't thought of it that way, but he would have a week ago. How could he not have realized? "I can't convince you the way you are," he whispered, almost to himself. "We just have to wait." They sat in silence for a while until, softly, Jordan did begin to cry.

"Don't cry," Evan said, wanting to cry himself. Guilt filled him from head to nub. "It *will* be okay. It isn't as bad as you think it is."

"What about my mom?" Jordan tried to quell his sobs, but instead he sobbed louder, tears filling his membranes. "My brother is dead. She won't have any kids left."

"Yes, she will," said Evan. He crawled closer to Jordan and folded his nubs over Jordan's crippled, folded hands. "You'll still be her son, even though you'll look different. My mother still loves me. Moms don't care what you look like."

"You mean . . . I can go back?" Jordan looked up at Evan, his head now a complete fishbowl.

"Of course. Not to stay, but you can visit." Maybe Jordan wouldn't be like Evan. Maybe he wouldn't care that it was a lie. Jordan sniffed again and breathed in. He stopped sobbing, and by the time Suzie came to relieve Evan, the tears had nearly drained.

TWENTY

THEY HAD ONLY TWO more nights to wait. During Ylander's shift he called down in excitement. Evan couldn't understand the message, since no words made it through the pipes, but Tret understood at once.

"He's changing!" he cried, and he jumped headfirst into the pipe, barely giving Evan a chance to grab on. When they slid out into the basement, all the Wuftoom had trouble keeping still. They were so excited that Evan realized they had never seen such a thing either.

Jordan was still on the floor, but he had somehow slipped from the ropes that held him, and he lay gasping, almost completely worm formed.

Evan remembered the pain and nearly cried out in sympathy.

But Jordan didn't cry out. He glared at the four Wuftoom. His body shook and his insides and outsides twisted, but he kept on glaring.

Evan wanted to scream, but he forced himself to watch. He thought this was the worst thing in the world, even worse than going through it all himself. Because this time he could have prevented it.

But watching Jordan go through the change was not the worst thing after all. The worst thing was staring into Jordan's eyes as, slowly, the glare of the human pupils changed into the white balls of the Wuftoom, and instead of glaring, they began to glow. Evan knew for certain that Jordan was not like him, that Jordan the human boy was gone.

Tret held out his nubs and pulled Jordan to standing. Jordan flexed his new limbs, watching the other Wuftoom with a mixture of curiosity and awe.

Without warning, Evan was filled with anger. It wasn't fair! Jordan had spent only a few days like that, not two years like Evan had. Why was it always harder for him? These feelings came out of nowhere, or from a place so deep, Evan had not wanted to face it. Wasn't he glad to still be human inside? To still have his mind if not his body? But Jordan didn't look sad. He looked curious, even excited. Why couldn't Evan just be happy? Why couldn't he just forget?

Jordan was putting his nub arm to his face, feeling for the features, stopping at the nose that was now flat, the eyebrows without hair, the eyes without lids. He didn't touch his mouth, staring instead at Evan's, a curious look glowing from his Wuftoom eyes.

"I can really see now," he said, sucking his lips in. He slowly pressed one leg into the ground and then the other, then pressed his arms together, mixing them, twisting them around each other.

"Welcome to the Wuftoom!" Tret cried. His wide grin

showed off his full fangs. He clapped Jordan in the Wuftoom way, nearly knocking him over.

Jordan grinned back.

"I am very sorry for the last few days," said Tret. "But you can see why we had to do it."

"I know," said Jordan. "It's all right." He rubbed his arms together and took a cautious step.

Evan remembered his first steps, how delighted he'd been that he could walk at all. Jordan couldn't possibly appreciate it.

"You've seen how we go down with the other new one," said Tret, nodding in Evan's direction. "So that's how we'll do it. I'll go down first and you grab on to me. Next will come Ylander. Then Suzie will follow with our older new one." Tret grinned at Evan. "Everybody got it?" He looked around the room.

Suzie and Ylander nodded. Tret headed for the pipe, and Jordan followed. As soon as Tret's head was in the drain, Jordan grabbed on to his legs, and he showed no surprise as he slowly squooshed up and followed Tret in. Evan found it difficult to look as Ylander grabbed on to Jordan and followed them down.

"That was hard for you?" asked Suzie, when they were alone.

"It seemed so easy for him," said Evan. "I wish it had been so easy for me." He wished so much more than that.

"Proems are different," said Suzie. "Nobody knows why. Maybe it's because humans are different.

"Some humans are born to be Wuftoom," she continued, when Evan said nothing in response. "We've always had a place in the dark. You and I, Tret and Ylander, and now your friend, we're all here because this is our home."

"So I had to step in that pit, and I had to lead Jordan into it?"

"It didn't have to happen any special way," said Suzie, "but it had to happen."

"Is this all in a book, like the Bible?" Evan asked. Suzie made it sound like a religion, with people being chosen and everyone playing a divine part.

"It's not from a book; it's just true. Everyone knows it's true. Like we know the sun will hurt us and the water feels cool. You know it too."

Evan didn't know it, but he saw that Suzie did. All of them must believe it, that they had a perfect right to do this to people. "I know," he said. But he would never believe he was chosen. He believed he'd had a terrible misfortune, and he would have done anything to take it back.

Reluctant, but trying not to act that way, he followed her down the pipes. They dropped heavily into the water. Tret, Ylander, and Jordan were already well ahead of them.

"How old were you when you became a Wuftoom?" Evan asked. He'd wondered that about all of them. Did you have to be a kid to be turned into one, or could it happen to anyone?

"I was eighteen," said Suzie.

"How long ago was that?"

"Seven years," she said.

"So you were the youngest before me?"

"The youngest Wuftoom," said Suzie. "Tret was only ten

when he was changed, but that was almost twenty years ago."

Ten. Tret had never had a chance to live a real human life. He didn't even know what he was missing, being down here. Evan had never had much of a life either. But Jordan, he would have had a lot of fun. Jordan had lost everything now. Evan stared up at the ceiling as he walked, trying to hide what he was thinking. For the first time he noticed a small floodlight, broken.

"Did you do that?" he asked, pointing.

"We destroy all the lights. Sometimes they try to repair them, but we just break them again," she answered. "Mostly they stop trying."

"And none of the people who come down here have ever seen you, or any of the things we eat?"

"No one would get within eyesight of a human!" Suzie sucked in her lips in an expression that he now knew signaled danger.

This was something Evan did know was true. Humans would kill them or dissect them. Even though he felt human inside, he knew he could never let one catch him. It didn't matter whether he was chosen like Suzie believed, or just horribly unlucky. It didn't matter what he or Jordan or Tret was missing. He could do nothing but slide onward, through the cool sewage toward the Wuftoom cave.

Master Rayden was glaring lasers through Tret. They were facing each other just inside the waterfall, both with their arms melted together and pressed against their bodies, giving the impression of puffed chests. Ylander and Jordan were standing behind Tret. They both watched Evan and Suzie as they approached. Ylander's eyes and mouth were sucked deep into his head, while Jordan pressed his arms together as if clasping his hands.

All of the other Wuftoom watched from their various places in the cavern.

"We got the proem," said Tret. "We needed him, and you know it."

"Without blindfolds?" Rayden growled.

"It's cruel and unnecessary," said Tret. "I didn't let them climb. *And* our first new one proved himself. He did his job as well as any Wuftoom could have, even better."

Rayden turned to Evan. He let his arms unbind from each other and rolled them both up, like yo-yos on strings. "You have done well, new one," he said. He let one of his arms snap to full length, poking it into Tret's middle. "We'll talk later. Get them settled in for the day." Rayden stalked off, splashing more than he needed to.

Tret turned to Evan and grinned wide. "See? No problem."

Evan had not noticed before, but one side of the cave was lined with concrete cinder blocks. Around the cave, the Wuftoom were carrying them out and piling them in the water.

"What are they doing?" Evan asked.

"This is how we sleep when we're at home," said Tret. "Come on, new ones. First day sleeping like real Wuftoom!"

He wrapped an arm around Jordan's back and led him toward where the other young ones were piling their blocks. Ylander, Evan, and Suzie followed.

Each Wuftoom set up four large concrete blocks. They put one down to sit on so the Wuftoom's body would be raised up in the water. They set the other three up as a back, so that each worm was sitting on a makeshift chair. Tret, Suzie, and Ylander helped Evan and Jordan set up their blocks.

"We need something hard to sleep on," Tret said, "because when we relax, we lose our shape. If we slept on a bed like a human, we might end up in a puddle. That's one of the reasons we slept in the pipes."

"What's the other reason?" asked Evan.

"The Vits," said Tret. "But don't worry. We're safe here. There's the water, which the Vits can't pass through, and two of us are always awake, keeping watch."

As Evan watched in amazement, the Wuftoom around him began going to sleep one by one. Their heads and backs molded around their blocks, as if they were almost melting into them.

"Go on, try it," said Ylander.

Jordan sat down on his blocks and leaned his head back. He didn't seem to be having any trouble with any of this. Why was it so easy for him? Evan pushed the jealousy back. He had to look like a good Wuftoom. *This is all normal. This is just how we sleep.*

He sat down on the lower block with a splash.

The others watched him with amusement.

"You have to relax into it," said Suzie. "Don't worry about letting go. The blocks will hold you." She sat down on her own blocks, right next to his.

Ylander and Tret and the others sat down on their blocks too. Jordan looked completely melted.

Evan sat there, still tense. He wanted to ask someone *how* he was supposed to relax, but even Tret seemed to already be sleeping, so he stared across the room. A hundred worms, all sleeping peacefully, melting into their blocks. The guards stood perfectly still at the mouth of the cave, facing outward.

Evan wondered what it would take to kill one. If you ripped off its membrane, would it lose its shape and go melting to the floor? Could you stab it or beat it, or would it just change its shape? What would it take to kill a hundred all at once? Would a bomb work? A fire? What if you took away their water?

Even as his mind turned over these plots, he realized he couldn't kill them. He had to stay belowground, and he didn't know how to survive here. He didn't know all the creatures and what they could do. He didn't know how to find food.

Could he learn all he needed in two more weeks, before he had to meet Foul?

It couldn't be real. There weren't any Vitflys. There weren't any worms. He wanted to close his eyes. To sleep and be free of this nightmare. To wake up in his bed at home, just a sick boy. But he couldn't close them, and the sleeping Wuftoom eyes stared back.

TWENTY-ONE

WE ARE WAITING, PROEM, the voice said. Suddenly, Evan could see. He had never even noticed that he had fallen asleep. Even though five more nights had passed since his first time sleeping on the blocks, he still wasn't really used to it. The cave was filled with sleeping Wuftoom, collapsed in near puddles against their blocks. There was no one awake.

I'm not a proem anymore, he thought.

Oh no, said the voice in his head. *You're a full-blooded worm now. Are you enjoying yourself? Drinking the pleasant nectar of human refuse?* The voice was familiar. Foul.

Evan started fully awake but didn't move. *Of course I'm not enjoying myself,* he snapped without speaking. *But I have to act like it. Otherwise, they'll be suspicious.*

Helping them retrieve their proem, said Foul. The word "proem" was long and slow and hissed. *We think you have gone over to their side.*

I haven't! Evan thought. How did they know? Were they watching him? He thought these things without meaning to think them. The Vitfly chittered in his mind. Evan could not see or hear it, but he knew its wings went flap, flap, flap.

You will not escape us.

I'm not trying to escape you, he thought. *I'm trying to get you what you want. But I don't know anything yet. They don't trust me because I don't have my name. I don't even know how to get back home.*

You will have all you need before the week is passed, Foul hissed.

What do you mean? Evan thought.

You will see. We will be waiting with her—The voice stopped abruptly.

With her? What do you mean? What are you doing to her? He screamed the thought as loud as he could think it, but there was no response. The Vit was gone.

Evan sat straight up in the cave, staring at the sleeping worms. The Vits were not supposed to be able to get into Wuftoom minds. But he was not a Wuftoom. He knew it as surely as he knew that the water flowing over his body stank. He was a human inside a Wuftoom body. The Vitflys knew that and used it. Only a human would care about his mother.

He calculated how much time had passed and how much he had left. It had been less than two weeks. That meant he should have one week more. But he didn't even know how to climb. How would he ever learn how to get home, much less find out how the Vitflys could get into the Wuftoom cave?

The Wuftoom began to stir. They rolled on their blocks, lifted, and slowly formed themselves.

His new family. Their lives depended on him not being weak. What if the Vits could read his mind? He had never read Jordan's mind, and the place where Foul's voice had been was gone. But it knew things.

Maybe he should tell Tret. He could let the Wuftoom decide for themselves how they would handle it. But what if they decided to keep him here? To them, Evan's mother didn't matter. Surely, that was what they'd do. Evan sat motionless as the others rose around him, turning it all over in his mind. He had to stay silent. He had to see what he could find out.

Tret, Suzie, Ylander, and Jordan approached. He could not make out their words, but their voices were deep and happy. Since returning from the old house, this group had always been with him. They never let him go anywhere or do anything alone.

"Why are you still sitting there?" asked Jordan. "Tonight we're going to learn how to use our packs and rods!"

Evan didn't recognize the voice that had briefly been his own. It was lower and growly now, and it said things the real Jordan never would have said. Then Evan remembered. Tret was planning to take them on a real hunt.

Evan and Jordan had been allowed to go with the Wuftoom when they hunted in the sewers, but so far they had not been allowed to go where most of the creatures were. It was considered too dangerous because the Vits hunted there too.

The Wuftoom spent nearly all their time hunting. Food was so scarce that often they ate only once a day, and it was a rare day when all the Wuftoom could be fed as well as Rayden and Olen and their cronies. Every night the hunters returned with their quarry—spiders, Mifties, Higgers, Orpas, and other things Evan learned were Gibbens, Nobs, Vays, and Crabs—and they tossed them in a pile for the cooks. The clan tried to maintain good cheer, especially in front of the nameless new ones, but there was no hiding the worry that filled the cave each day when the hunters came home with less.

Evan got the impression that new ones normally were not allowed to hunt so soon, but the Wuftoom needed all the bodies they could get.

Jordan was grinning like an excited child. The others were also smiling, as if they were about to embark on a great game. Evan knew this was his chance to learn more, to come closer to giving the Vitflys what they wanted, but this thought did not excite him. He found himself unable to move and continued to sit rigid on his blocks.

"Still hates waking up," said Tret, clapping him. The blow pushed Evan forward, and in catching his balance, he was forced to stand. "No time for sleeping in! Tonight we get you ready to leave the sewers. To go where Wuftoom really belong!"

"If we belong there," said Evan, "then why do we stay here?" He was annoyed at Tret's happiness.

"Not for long, new one! Not for long!" Evan shivered at what had been Olen's refrain. But Tret didn't notice. He was even more exuberant than usual. Eagerly, he showed Evan and Jordan the weapons they would use. They looked like melted plastic rods from the outside. Their surfaces were lined and twisted, bumpy and mottled. But Evan had watched the Wuftoom as they made them, and he knew what they were made of: membrane, from the Wuftoom's precious stores.

"Each one of you will get his own," said Tret proudly.

Jordan gasped with pleasure. His whole body puffed out and

in again. Evan tried to imitate him, but he felt worse than ever. The real Jordan would not be excited. Tret solemnly handed a rod to each of them, and they wrapped them with their worm arms, testing their weight. Jordan tossed his and caught it, then tossed it and caught again, his arms folding around it like he was born to handle it with Wuftoom nubs.

It was so much like how he'd tossed a basketball that Evan's heart skipped a beat.

Jordan didn't seem to miss basketball. He didn't seem to miss his mother, whom he had cried over so recently. He didn't seem to miss the sun, or school, or friends. He hunted the water creatures with the same strength and agility he had used for everything human, yet everything human was forgotten. Was he still in there at all?

Evan tried to put it out of his mind and copy Jordan's technique. He knew that even as a Wuftoom, he had no hope of matching Jordan's skill, but he had to learn the best he could.

Tret started explaining how they worked. "The packs stay on your back at all times outside the waterways. No exceptions, understand?"

The new ones nodded. Because the membrane was too precious, the packs were made of other creatures, their skins sewn together with the strong hair that grew from Gibbens' feet. They were lined with Nob intestines for watertightness and filled with water before each hunting trip.

"The thicker end syncs to the opening," said Tret, and he swiftly attached his rod to his pack with one arm, so fast that

Evan couldn't see exactly what he did. "You have to be able to reload without looking, without even thinking about it." He pulled the rod swiftly from the pack again and held it out toward Jordan, in fighting form.

Evan watched nervously, feeling like a useless human. When he wasn't able to do it, would they know?

"The trick is not to think too much about it," Tret continued. "The hole will be there. It's protected on the inside by membrane. The water won't come out, but your rod will go in, smooth as a Miftie down a tired throat. Let's get this down before we actually load up."

For the next hour the new ones practiced, tossing their rods back and drawing them forward and from this arm to that arm, with Tret circling, giving direction. Since changing, Evan hadn't yet experienced real fatigue, but the repetition of the movement made his arms ache from somewhere deep. Not quite like muscle soreness, the pain seemed to seep from his arms into his body like warm liquid, almost too hot.

Though Jordan learned it faster, Evan was surprised to find that before his arms finally gave out, he was connecting the rod with the membrane nearly every time. He was doing so well, he earned a big clap on the back from Tret.

"Good job, new one! Those Vits are no match for you!"

Evan smiled at him. He was exhilarated in his fatigue. He was learning something he could use to defend himself. And he was learning that maybe the Wuftoom could all defend themselves. Maybe the Vitflys wouldn't win no matter what he did.

He sat down in the water to rest, but Jordan was already

tossing his rod back into his pack, getting ready for what came next. Evan's arms were shaking, but he got back up again. He was not going to give up before he learned to shoot.

"The Vits can't pass through running water," Tret explained, "but that doesn't mean it hurts them. It just acts as a barrier. Normally they don't get hurt by it because they know it's there and they avoid running up against it, like you wouldn't run smack into a wall. But in battle, you can get them!" He grinned and his fangs showed.

His arm was twisted tight around his rod, and for the first time Evan realized how strong Tret was. If Tret had been human, he would have been big with muscles. As a Wuftoom, his membranes were tight and his arms rubbery and flexible.

"If you can get a good stream in front of them while they're flying hard, it'll be just like watching them smack into that wall." Tret was clearly excited, but he made his expression serious. "It's a good feeling, but you're not ready for that yet. You have to learn how to defend yourselves. How to keep them off you while you retreat." His shriveled lips twisted as he said it, as if the word *retreat* was hard to say. "First you have to load."

With their packs now full of water, Evan and Jordan practiced. It was surprisingly hard. There was a special way you had to twist the membrane to get the water to flow into the rod. You had to get it just right, or the water would just slosh, with barely any of it getting in. That was when Evan got the rod to hit the pack at all. He was so tired that half the time he would miss, and when he did manage to hit the pack right, he would get the membrane twist all wrong.

Even Jordan had some difficulty with it, but after a while he was getting the hang of it, and Tret stopped the practice to teach them both to shoot.

Fortunately, shooting was much easier than loading. It just took a certain amount of pressure on the membrane, which could easily be done with any Wuftoom's strength. Still, Evan marveled to watch Tret do it. His whole arm twisted around his rod, and he drew it back without strain, hitting the pack right on, twisting his arms so smoothly that it was hard to notice they had moved, thrusting the rod back and letting a stream of water go.

The young ones had set up targets in the corner of the cave. They were dead creature skins, hanging from the ceiling by Gibben hair. Tret shot the streams in front of them at an angle, so fast that the skins blew in the wind and were thrust back. He grinned as he did it, and Evan imagined the real things, hissing and screaming as they were tossed backward, falling like bricks into the water.

Evan was determined to learn it. Before the end of the night, he was loading almost as well as Jordan, and the next night he made his first good shots. He knew he was learning fast, but it was not fast enough. He needed to learn more before it was too late. He had to find his way home.

His mother's face stayed in his mind, and over it, the flap, flap, flapping of the Vits. He didn't hear Foul's voice again, but he didn't need it to remind him.

Jordan was obviously as eager as Evan to go, although for him it seemed to be fun and exciting.

"Tomorrow!" Jordan whispered to Evan when they had a break.

"I think so too," said Evan.

Tret had been showing his fangs, eagerly sliding around all night, unable to keep still. And sure enough, the next evening Tret and the other young ones woke Evan and Jordan early, smiling with their fangs out.

TWENTY-TWO

THE NEW ONES NERVOUSLY FIDDLED with their packs, checking and rechecking to make sure they were secure on their backs and practicing their load technique. Evan was so nervous, he missed the first few times he tried, but when Tret laughed and told him to relax, Evan steadied himself and was able to hit the spot again.

"Not to disappoint you," said Tret, "but it's unlikely that we'll run across any Vits tonight. We're not going out too far today. But it's always possible, so don't let your guard down."

Jordan gripped his rod and gave a fang-filled grin.

Evan could not share his excitement. He actually knew one. What would the Vits think if they knew he had a weapon? Would they be convinced that he had turned against them? But he had no choice. He wanted to scream to them in his mind, *I have to! I have to learn so I can do what you want!* But there was no one in his mind but him.

Jordan followed Ylander and another young Wuftoom named Blottix out of the cave. They were set up in groups of three. Evan was to go with Tret and Suzie.

"Good luck!" Jordan said to Evan as he passed on with his team.

"You, too," said Evan, smiling without meaning to. He couldn't help but think of school, and how Jordan had never spoken two words to him when they were boys, and despite himself, he felt a surge of pride to have been noticed. It blocked out his confusion for a moment. It came back only a minute later.

"First you have to learn to climb," said Tret. "The old Nob's allowing it because we need hunters." He grinned.

At first Evan nearly leaped with excitement. This was what he had been waiting for. Yet if this meant that he could travel, then he would have to travel. He would have to do something, make a choice that he did not want to make. A great part of him would have preferred to remain helpless. His whole body pumped as Tret spoke.

"I'll still go first, and Suzie will still go after you, so you can't get lost or fall backward, but this time we won't link up unless you need it."

Evan nodded, holding all his feelings in.

"The trick is to grip the pipe walls with your membrane. It takes practice because your first tendency is to slide. You do want to slide; you just want to be able to direct yourself. You have to use your strength to draw yourself up. Let's practice against this wall."

Tret leaned himself against the wall of the large pipe and compressed into traveling form. His legs glued to his body. His arms stuck up over his head, melting until his head was giant and deformed. He held his rod above him, with both arms wrapped around it. Then his back began to fold the pack into itself, so that the pack finally sank into him completely, and Tret was standing nearly flat against the wall.

Evan stared in amazement, his back itching in sympathy.

"It might seem like it's just a kind of skin, but I'm sure you've noticed by now, membrane doesn't just protect you. It's our biggest organ, and the strongest, too."

Evan hadn't noticed. It had never done much except hang on him.

Tret seemed to read what he was thinking. "You haven't had a reason to really use it yet. It doesn't come from your arms or your legs. It comes from your center, from what really makes you a Wuftoom. That's the part of you that can control it."

Evan knew that his insides had changed around. He knew his organs had changed, so that most things seemed to flow through his whole body, like his breathing and his heartbeat. But there still was something in his core, something that stayed in one place. He thought that must be what Tret meant.

"You feel it?" Tret asked.

Evan nodded.

"Okay, once you've got yourself ready, like you see me now, you concentrate with that part of you. You send your energy, your Wuftoom core, out to the membrane that you need to use. That's the top of your arms to start, and then the rest of your body as you slide through. You make it ripple from one part to the next, so you'll grip when you need to and slide when you need to."

This sounded too hard to Evan, but he tried to hold back his doubts. He had to learn this. He stood next to Tret and leaned himself against the wall. He lifted his arms with his rod over his head and tried to relax into it, letting his limbs collide and mix. The pack tickled as it started to fold into his back, then burned. He jerked forward.

"Just let it go," said Suzie. "Let it fall in. Let your body absorb the water. Don't worry, it's made specially for this. Just let it sink."

Evan held tight as his back folded slowly around it. He felt himself bloat with it.

"Good! Now try to move your membranes," Suzie went on. "Don't think about it too hard. Let it go and concentrate on your center."

Evan tried to do as she said. For the thousandth time he felt that everything would be easier if he could just close his eyes. But they stared forward at the other wall, a rounded concrete monster covered in green slime. He twisted his arms, and Suzie frowned.

"Your arms shouldn't move," she said, "only your membrane. Your body follows the membrane."

Evan took a deep breath with his whole body and stared past Suzie at the wall. He tried to focus on his core like Tret said. He knew it was there. It really was the part of him that was Wuftoom, the part he'd been fighting for weeks now. He'd done everything he could to pretend it didn't exist, and when he did notice it, it was an illness. It made him love to eat dark creatures and fear the sunlight like he used to fear the dark.

It's just to get through the pipes, he thought. *I can fight it again after that. After I learn how to get back.*

He took another breath and let his consciousness fall into it. The view of the wall was still there, but it became unimportant background. He felt springy, but not soft. He felt a coolness on the outside, and on the inside, a growing heat. He imagined the pipe he was about to go up. He'd been up them many times attached to another Wuftoom's legs. He felt the coolness of the pipe against the coolness of his body and imagined pressing himself against it and, slowly, sliding upward.

He lifted and lifted. Then suddenly he was really seeing the wall again, and Suzie was standing in front of him, a big grin on her face.

"Did I do it?" he asked, breathing deeply. It took a lot of energy, even just standing there pretending.

"You did it!" said Tret proudly. "It took me a lot longer to get that!"

Evan smiled uneasily. He felt on fire, his eyes now sharper, searching the water for creatures, watching the pipes and the cracks in case any came out. He desperately wanted to hunt, but he didn't want to at all.

"No time to waste, then," said Tret, and he pushed his head up into the pipe and started sliding.

Evan hesitated.

"Don't worry," said Suzie. "I'll be right behind you."

Evan pushed his rod into the pipe, then his arms and then his head. Now that he was pressed so tight, he was less distracted by his open eyes. He settled back into his core, and he felt himself moving up, slowly, but up. He could feel Tret ahead of him even though they weren't connected, so when Tret made a turn, Evan followed easily. He was so slow that Suzie bumped him a couple times, but he never fell back into her.

After a few minutes they began heading steadily down, which was easier than going up. Still, he got slower and slower as they went, and by the time they dropped out of the last pipe, he was gasping for breath. For the first time he felt his membranes ache. He had not known they could ache. It felt like an arm being pulled out from the shoulder a thousand times, all over his body.

"What a Wuftoom!" Tret said, grinning at Evan from above him, since Evan had dropped, exhausted, to the ground. His pack was sticking partway out, and he shook it all the way. He gasped as the air sucked it from his body.

"In and out is hard," Tret said, "but it will get easier, I promise." Tret and Suzie sat down next to Evan while he recovered his strength. Evan noticed that they, too, gasped as their packs released.

They were not in the sewers anymore. They were in a tunnel carved out of the ground, just barely tall enough for them to stand in and not wide enough to walk in side by side. The walls were unevenly cut and dirt dripped from the ceilings, landing in small and large piles. No human had made this tunnel, and no animal, either. He couldn't think of any dark creatures who could have made it.

"Who made this?" he asked.

"The Boomtulls," said Tret. "The same race that made the

Birch the Vits stole. They had large claws and they were very strong."

"Were? What happened to them?"

"They left," said Tret. "We're too young to remember, but the old ones say they left for a far-off place, somewhere without many humans. They hated humans with a passion. They would dig up into human houses and catch them while they were sleeping. They could go into the humans' minds, and they used their skill to give them nightmares. Adults, children, babies, the Boomtulls wanted to destroy them all. They'd drive people crazy." Tret paused thoughtfully. "I guess all the dark creatures think about doing it," he continued, "but we Wuftoom need humans for proems. The Boomtulls drove many to their deaths."

"They could get into people's minds?" Evan asked, his heart pumping. "But not Wuftoom's?"

"I'm told the Boomtulls could," said Tret, "though they refrained because of a truce between our races. But don't worry; the Vits can't even get into humans. The scholars say the Vitfly minds are different. They're more like flies than either Wuftoom or human."

Evan desperately wanted to know more about this, but he couldn't let Tret know that he was wrong.

"What the Vits gave you, they can't use," said Tret. He looked solemnly at Evan, then put his arm on Evan's shoulder kindly. "They can't hurt you. If they want to hurt us, they will have to fight us in the flesh." He gripped his rod and twisted his strong arms around it with a grimace of his shriveled lips.

"I won't do what they want," Evan blurted. "I won't help them. I promise. I want to help you destroy them!" As he said it, he knew it was true. He wanted nothing more than to destroy the Vitflys. It was a part of him like his membrane and his nubs. He wanted it more than anything. Almost.

"We know that!" Tret smiled and squeezed his back. "It is not Wuftoom nature, what they want. They misunderstand us."

Evan's heart raced. They did not know the Vits had talked to him in his mind. They did not know how much human was left and how different he was. He didn't want to be different. He didn't want to care about his mother. He wanted to stop caring just like Jordan had. He wanted to cry in frustration, but he willed himself to remain calm.

"Why did the Boomtulls leave?" he asked.

"The humans caught one and killed it," Suzie replied. "They were going to dissect it. But the others rescued the body and they all left."

"Is that what we'd do if the humans caught one of us?"

Tret shook his head. "I don't know. There's been a lot of talk, but so far we just hope it never happens."

They sat silently a few more minutes. Evan breathed in the damp, earthy air. It was a thousand times sweeter than the sewers. He had thought that the Wuftoom were suited to the sewers, with their lack of smell and their sense of touch adapted to the feel of the water. But now he knew that he was wrong. He knew they were meant to live here, in the earth. And knowing that, he fully realized how afraid they were of the Vitflys, to remain cooped up in their man-made slums.

No one said anything, but he could tell the others were also drinking in the air. Finally, Tret stood up, and Suzie and Evan followed. Tret checked his pack and lifted his rod.

"What are we looking for?" asked Evan as they started moving single file down the tunnel.

"Nobs," said Tret. Nobs were furry little creatures that looked like rodents, but they had no eyes. Their heads had empty holes on them where the eyes should be, and what the holes did for the Nobs, nobody knew. Evan had never seen one living, and now he knew why. "They travel in burrows that cross the Boomtull tunnels. If you look closely, you'll see the openings on the walls. They appear closed up, but there'll be an indent that doesn't quite match with the surrounding walls. Sometimes the Nobs cross our path, but if not, we reach up into the holes and grab them."

"If they're intelligent, why don't they hide?"

Tret snorted. "'Intelligent' is pushing it. Have you ever tried to talk to one?" He looked at Suzie and she smiled meanly, one fang showing.

"They only know a few words," she said. "Barely better than a rat."

Suddenly, Tret stopped and punched his left arm into the wall. It sank through the dirt and out of sight. His shoulder, which really wasn't a shoulder but was just the place where the arm met the Wuftoom's body, twisted slightly back and forth. A minute later his arm bounced back and out, a little ratlike creature wriggling in his grip. With his other arm, Tret reached out and broke the little creature's neck. He handed it to Suzie, who put it in a pouch inside Tret's pack.

"See?" said Tret. "Not too bright."

Evan felt a little sick, yet desperately hungry at the same time. They had not eaten since the night before.

The three continued down the tunnel, Tret and Suzie punching into the wall every few yards. After watching them awhile, Evan easily began to see where the holes were. It was so easy, it might have been instinct. The strangest thing was that when he stopped to examine an indentation closely, it seemed to disappear. He felt sure he couldn't have seen it at all as a human.

Punching into the wall was easy too. His arm reached into the hole and stretched. He could somehow sense the creature's heat, and when he came close, his arm pressed against one side of the hole and swiftly moved in front of it, folding the creature back and pulling it out of the hole.

The holes where its eyes should have been faced Evan's eyes, and he got the eerie impression that even without eyes the thing could see.

"Back!" the thing said. Its voice was a quiet squeak. It wriggled in his arm, but it was no match. "Back! Back!" it squeaked.

Seeing that Evan was doing nothing but staring, Tret came back to him and broke the creature's neck. Evan put it gently in his pack, trying not to show his grief. It was the first time he'd heard another creature talk, outside of the Wuftoom and the Vitflys. And it had been afraid. He was sure he would never get used to it, and he didn't want to.

He knew he couldn't let Suzie and Tret see what he was feeling. He felt everything Wuftoom in him pulling him toward the Nob holes, raising visions of how good they'd taste. He'd had Nobs many times in the past weeks. They weren't the tastiest of all the creatures, but they fed the hunger that was getting stronger every day. He knew that even though he'd heard one talk, he wouldn't be able to resist it when it was served at dinner. He almost couldn't resist eating one now.

This went on for quite some time, with the three Wuftoom walking, punching, killing, and moving on. The tunnel twisted this way and that and went down and down, but its appearance never changed. Despite his confusion and disgust, Evan found it tedious.

But there was one good part. It was the feel of the earthy air in his body, so fresh and good compared to the air in the sewers above. He had never felt anything so fresh, not even as a human outside in the open air.

After a long while the Wuftoom came to a fork. Suddenly, Evan heard a noise. *Flap. Flap. Flap.*

TWENTY-THREE

Tret whipped out his rod and loaded in an instant. Evan's arms shook, and he missed the pack his first time. He felt Suzie grab his rod and direct it in. Then they came flying out. Three of them, their wings buzzing, hissing, fangs first. Tret took a shot in the path of one, right over Evan's head, but the bug dived and the water dripped onto Evan.

Evan raised his rod, but they were so fast, he didn't know where to point it.

Suzie shot in front of the Vit as it came back up again, and it fell backward as if it had slammed against a wall. It was dazed and started falling, but it caught itself in midair and flapped its wings. Its yellow eyes glared at Evan, whose rod was raised, but who could do nothing while it stood still.

The other two dived at Tret, and Tret hit one full on with his rod, but the Vit grabbed on to the rod with its claws. Tret shot at the second, but the creature deftly dodged and made a dive for Suzie. She shot again, but missed it too.

It landed on her back and dug its claws in. She screamed, twisting and turning to try to shake it off. Evan turned around and hit the Vitfly with his rod. He hit Suzie as well so that she fell forward, but the Vitfly was dislodged.

A stream of water came around Evan, and the creature screamed as it fell backward, flipping over and over in the air until it was finally upright, several yards down the passage.

Suddenly, the one clinging to Tret's rod jumped free. It screeched a deafening, high-pitched hiss and flew straight at Evan's face. Both of the other Vits had recovered, and they, too, flew straight at Evan. He shot wildly in front of him, but he wasn't even close to cutting off their path. Tret and Suzie shot water on both sides of him, but the creatures twisted and turned and screeched, dodging the streams. One of the Vits landed on Evan's head, one on his shoulder, and one on his back. Their clawed feet tore through his membrane and he screamed, dropped his rod, and collapsed onto the ground.

It was like no pain he'd experienced before. It was not like cut skin; it was like cut sinews and bone. Though their claws barely pierced through, it felt like his skin was being ripped from his body.

Evan screamed and screamed. From far off he felt rods beating his back, but the beating seemed to make the claws dig in deeper, the hissing screeches louder. And then came the worst thing he'd felt or thought he ever would feel. Three sets of fangs dug all at once into his back. He screamed and rolled, but the three Vits were much stronger than he was.

All of a sudden, one was gone. Then the second, then the third. The pain was still there, but Evan rolled. He tried to push himself to standing, but his arms slid helplessly along the ground and he lay there, twisting. One of the bugs was silent on the ground, another was flying back down the passage it had come from, and Tret was wrestling a third.

It screeched and clawed at Tret's arms, but he held its wings firmly. Suddenly, he threw it toward its passage and Suzie shot a stream of water right into its path. It hit the wall and fell, silent next to its comrade. Tret and Suzie fell on the two, breaking their bodies apart to be sure they were dead.

They shoved the dead Vits into their packs and pulled Evan up. He couldn't stand by himself, and they had to drag him down the passage. No one spoke. Tret's face was grim, and his grip was hard around Evan's arm, nearly squeezing it to nothing.

Evan had never known a Wuftoom to move so fast, but they made it back to the drop-off point in minutes. Tret pulled Evan's pack and rod from him, and Evan grabbed feebly for Suzie's legs as she jumped in. The pipes scraped angrily against his exposed flesh as he went up, and he would have screamed, but the pressure of compression on his body forced his silence.

As he fell into the sewage, Suzie and Tret collapsed around him. They supported his back so he didn't fall all the way in, and he felt himself being lifted and half pushed, half pulled through the waterfall and into the cave. Several Wuftoom met them, and soon they were covering his back with some kind of goo.

Whatever they were doing, they had to touch his membrane and pull it together, and it hurt nearly as much as it had when the bugs had clawed him, but he pursed his lips and stopped himself from crying out.

He woke up some time later to find that he'd been moved to his sleeping blocks and that Tret and the other young ones were anxiously watching him. As he awoke, he heard tense voices.

"Where did you take him?" asked an angry voice.

"We took him to the Yellow Passage to hunt for Nobs. It should have been perfectly safe. We haven't seen a Vitfly there in years." It was Tret's defiant voice.

"You must have attracted their attention!" said the first voice. Then there was another voice that seemed to come at the same time.

We've never tasted anything so sweet, Foul hissed. It brought Evan totally awake. He saw that the Wuftoom arguing with Tret was Olen. Both looked at him and turned his way.

"How are you?" asked Tret. His mouth was turned down and his white eyes glowed sad and sorry. Evan hadn't known how expressive Wuftoom eyes could be. Olen's eyes were blazing with anger. Evan would have shrunk back from them if he could have fallen any further. As it was, he was a crumpled mess, soggy against his blocks.

So sweet we think only of more.

"Look at him!" Olen cried. "He can't even talk! I told you it was too soon to bring him out. We aren't starving badly enough to take these kinds of risks." Olen gave Tret one last glare before sloshing angrily across the cave, clearly heading for Rayden and their gang.

Tret shook his head sadly. "He did tell me not to take you,

but not out of worry for this. It was because you do not yet have your name. 'We must be sure that every bit of human has been changed.'" Tret mimicked Olen's raspy growl.

Evan found himself unable to speak, but he shook his head slowly.

But it's not changed, is it, proem? We can taste it in your flesh.

"I know it's hard to talk. I got scratched by one of those bugs too. A long time ago." Tret turned so his back was facing Evan and pointed to a spot on his lower back. Evan had never noticed it before, but the membrane was lumpy and knotted. "It was in a low tunnel, supposedly much more dangerous than Yellow. We were low on food then, too, and getting desperate. They had me down flat, and if it hadn't been for Ylander . . ." He shook his head.

"You saved me," Evan whispered. "You and Suzie . . ." Evan struggled to try to get upright, but it was too much effort and he fell back again.

"She's resting," said Tret. "She got clawed a little too." He gave a long, full-bodied sigh. "I'm sorry I got you into that. I thought it was the safest passage. The very safest."

"What about the others? Did they get back?" Evan asked.

"They're fine," Tret said. "No trouble."

They didn't promise us, Foul hissed. *They didn't have a bargain.*

"They were going for me," said Evan, frantic. "I know it. They want me to betray you, but I won't. They threatened to eat me if I didn't. That's why they came for us. I know it." Tret's strong nubs held him on his blocks.

"They can't come in here," he said. "You're safe while you're in here." Tret's sorry eyes were intense and sincere. "We're not going to let them get at you again. Okay?"

Evan shuddered a little, but he stopped fighting. He'd seen the way the water affected them. Tret was right. They couldn't get in here.

Who's protecting your mother, proem? We can eat creatures light and dark.

I know, thought Evan. *I'm still trying. That was the first time I've gotten out of the sewers. Now, thanks to you, they might never let me out again!* Evan willed himself to think no other thoughts.

You will have all you need, proem. You will have your name now.

So that was it. They had attacked him so the worms would trust him.

It won't work! He cried it in his mind, but somehow he knew that Foul was gone. It hadn't heard him. It didn't care.

"It doesn't matter what Master Olen thinks," Tret went on. "Rayden's already agreed. You're a real Wuftoom now, you and the other one. You'll get your names tonight." Tret smiled, but his eyes were still sad. "You've given up a lot for it, but you won't be called 'new one' anymore. You'll be one of us. One of the young ones." His smile broadened proudly, and Evan froze. This was exactly what the Vits wanted.

My name is Evan, Evan thought. *I'm still human! Don't trust me!* He found the words as difficult to hold back as his heart-beat, but he kept them in.

"What will it be?" he asked, his voice a painfully small rasp.

Tret shook his head. "It can't be revealed until the ceremony, when all the Wuftoom are gathered. It's a tradition we've been missing for seven years."

Evan tried to smile, but he did not know what to feel. He needed this to escape, but he did not want the Vits to get what they wanted. How did he even know he could trust them? He hadn't seen his mother in two weeks. He had no idea if she was even alive. They could have eaten her already and might just be lying. He sank back into his blocks. The confusion exhausted him.

"Just rest for now," said Tret. "I'll wake you when it's time." And Evan fell back into a restless sleep.

TWENTY-FOUR

EVAN WOKE TO THE SOUND of Wuftoom moving. The water sloshed around him as they gathered in the cave. As his vision cleared, he saw some Wuftoom carrying the large membrane bowl. It was used for big meals, when they all ate together, when there was something to celebrate. As he watched, young ones surrounded him. Suzie and Ylander were front and center and Jordan was nearby. They were all smiling at him like he was their best friend. He stared back, dazed.

"Can you stand up?" asked Suzie. Her voice was quiet and concerned but filled with a brimming excitement.

"I don't know," Evan said. "I'll try. Are you all right?"

"I'm fine," she said, grinning. "A couple of little Vit nicks never hurt anyone!" The other young ones laughed in approval. But Evan had seen the Vit dig its claws into her back. He knew she must be in pain.

Evan slowly sucked himself together until he was sitting steady on his blocks. Then, with Suzie's arms twisted around his and with her doing most of the work, he managed to get up to standing. Cheers went up from those around him. Without thinking, he had to smile. His back was a giant wound, burning in places, aching in others. But he could tell he was on his way to healing. He knew that the membranes that had been sliced open were connecting again.

The young ones helped him forward until they were near the fire, and they all sat in the water, which felt soothing on Evan's back. The noise of excited whispers filled the cave. Clearly nothing so exciting had happened in a long time. On one side of him were Suzie and Ylander, on the other were Jordan and some other young ones. Jordan rubbed his lips together.

"What are they like?" Jordan whispered, sounding half frightened, half awed.

Evan looked at him uneasily. "Ugly and mean," he answered.

"Wow. But you fought them off!"

"I didn't," said Evan. "Tret and Suzie did. I couldn't even load without Suzie's help." Jordan still looked admiring, and Evan couldn't help but feel proud. Jordan Bates admired him!

"I'm sure I couldn't have either," said Jordan.

Evan thought that Jordan probably would have been able to load and hit the target, but he could see that Jordan was being sincere. "You're a good shot," Evan said. "You don't have to worry."

"No, I'm not," said Jordan. "And look what they did to you even with two others. What if they caught one of us alone?" His eyes glowed with fearful excitement.

"We don't travel alone," said Evan. "That's what Tret said. We always hunt in groups of three." Jordan pressed his lips together harder, and Evan hadn't convinced himself. He changed the subject. "What do you think this ceremony's all about? What will our names be?"

"Wait, didn't you bring back the dead Vitflys?" asked Jordan. "Do you think we'll get to try them?"

Evan had tried to keep it from his mind, but the craving to eat them had been with him since he first saw their sharp fangs coming at him. It had grown even as they whispered threats into his mind, and now that someone had said it out loud, it filled him from his membrane to his inner flesh.

In unison, the new ones bared their fangs and caught each other's glowing eyes. They craned their necks to see, but they saw only a mix of other creatures frying. Evan saw a great many spiders, Nobs, Higgers, and Orpas. It must have been an especially good day for Nobs, because they leaped high and often from the bowl.

Rayden got up and moved toward the center, where he stood not far from Evan and the other young ones. As he raised his nubs, the cave fell into expectant silence.

"Brothers!" he cried, his voice echoing throughout the cave. "This is a great day!"

The Wuftoom growled their cheers.

"We all know what happened in the Yellow Passage."

Uneasy whispers.

"But instead of shame and empty membrane, our young ones came back with two dead Vits!"

This time the cheering was wild. Evan's chest swelled and his mouth watered. He imagined their blood, their crunch.

"Through the valor of Tret, and Suzie, and the first new

one, who will get his name tonight, we have our enemy to eat!" More cheers and shouts. "Clear the bowl!" At this the Wuftoom in charge of cooking deftly dumped the roasted creatures into waiting arms.

Then Tret came forward from behind the bowl. He was carrying the Vitflys, one wrapped in each arm. Evan and Jordan exchanged eager, bloodthirsty looks. Tret held the Vits high above his head as the entire Wuftoom clan went wild. Evan joined in the growls, and all those around him were just as loud. Many were standing, but Evan couldn't get his legs to work. It was hard enough just sitting up. His body was on fire.

Tret tossed the Vits into the bowl, and they jumped and crackled. The smell wafted through the cave, making the Wuftoom rabid.

"Remove!" shouted Rayden, and the cooks pulled the Vitflys out. They handed the Vits to Rayden, who solemnly received them. From somewhere in the water, he pulled out an instrument of membrane. Evan had never seen one, but its use became apparent. Rayden raised it up and brought it down on the first Vit, and it sliced neatly in two. Rayden deftly chopped off the claws and fangs and soon had cut the two Vitflys into four pieces.

"For the young heroes and the new ones to be named!" Rayden cried. Cheers went up, but also shouts of disappointment. Though they knew there was not enough to go around, each Wuftoom craved a piece more than logic could stem.

Evan and Jordan were nearly fainting with excitement, as was Suzie. He felt her body shaking next to his. Rayden solemnly approached with the pieces and Tret followed. First Rayden held out a piece to Tret, who took it eagerly. He held it steady, but his fangs were showing and his body heaved. Next came Suzie, then Evan, then Jordan. All held on to their pieces, desperate to feed.

"Eat!" cried Rayden.

Evan bit in. It was like all the other dark creatures combined, but more. It was saltier, bloodier, meatier, more rich, more sweet. The blood dripped down his throat. The crunch echoed from his teeth into his membrane. It was ecstasy, and before he knew it, it was gone. He wanted more. His fangs pressed against his tongue and his teeth chattered.

He watched the juice dripping from Jordan's mouth and saw him rub it off with his arm and lick it. Tret was doing the same, a great fire in his eyes. A growl came from the crowd, a cheer, but one full of jealousy and greed.

The Wuftoom servers passed the other creatures around. Evan also got half a spider, which was as much by itself as most received. But it wasn't good enough. It was only a hollow shadow of the taste and crunch and blood of Vitfly. Evan wasn't sure he would ever like his food again.

After a voracious spell of eating, Rayden stood up. "And now for the names!" he cried, pointing one arm at Evan. "Who stands with this Wuftoom?"

Olen moved toward Evan from the crowd. He grabbed one of Evan's arms and Tret grabbed the other, and the two Wuftoom pulled him upright and through the waiting Wuftoom to the center. They had to hold on to him to keep him from falling. His back burned as he rose fully out of the water.

"This new one was marked by the Vits tonight!" Rayden bellowed. "Yet here he stands!"

The crowd cheered.

"He stands with the one who protected and retrieved him, Master Olen!" More cheers. "And the one who has trained him and fought the Vitflys by his side. Tret!"

The cheers for Tret were even louder.

"He stands before us a full Wuftoom. Never again to crave the sunlight. Never again to eat dumb animals or drink in the upper air. Never to be alone, without us, his brothers!"

Evan's legs wanted to sink. His arms wanted to drop and take his body with them, but he held on, twisting his arms tightly around Tret's and Olen's. He stared out at the Wuftoom. Their nubs were raised in cheers, fangs showing in smiles, eyes glowing with welcome.

"He was long to change," Rayden called, "but quick to show his mettle. He has brought another into our clan and fought our enemy with valor." More growls. "And so . . ." Rayden extended his nub in a gesture toward Evan.

Tret spoke. "He will be named Brode!"

The room erupted into shouting. It was a surge of approval and welcome for Evan. He smiled weakly, but it was too much. Though they stayed in their places, Evan felt as if they were moving, running toward him, arms raised, fangs out. He wanted to hold up his arms to stop them coming, and without thinking, he loosened his grip on Tret and Olen. He started to fall, but both worms caught him and held him tight.

"Brode!" echoed Rayden.

Lighter cheers came, and Tret and Olen pulled Evan back to his seat. He collapsed in the water and let it flow over him. Olen showed his fangs and gave Evan's arm a twist. Olen was pleased! Tret grinned and clapped him before pulling Jordan from his seat.

Jordan didn't need help, and he slid with Tret, Suzie, and Ylander to the center. He was given the name Rutgi, and when he returned to his spot, he was glowing with excitement. He began calling Evan "Brode" at once. Evan wondered if he would ever hear his real name again.

Jordan—Rutgi—was a full Wuftoom, with no more craving for the sunlight, just like Rayden had said. He had been more Wuftoom on his first day than Evan would ever be. Jordan was Rutgi now. But who was Evan? He craved both the sunlight and the air beneath the deepest earth.

I'm Evan, he thought. *And Jordan is Jordan, even if he doesn't know it.* Evan wondered what Jordan's mother and father were doing now. How long would they search for their last son? At that moment Evan vowed to remember for both of them. He would remember Jordan's parents, Angela, even Jordan's dead brother whom Evan had never met. *I'll tell them what happened someday,* he thought.

Tret stood up and called for silence. He was bigger than average, and although his voice was of normal strength, the room quieted somewhat at his call.

"Brothers!" Tret cried loudly. His voice carried from wall to wall, and the room hushed further. "Today the Vits came closer to us than they have in years. They attacked us without fear!"

Someone let out an angry growl.

"I, too, am angry," Tret went on. "And I do not like to admit fear. But today we must admit it."

The cave was totally silent. Everyone waited for Tret to speak.

"They have come to our safest hunting ground. No one can say they will not come here next." There was sloshing, but the Wuftoom remained quiet. "All know we are on the brink of war. But I say we are not close enough." There was more silent sloshing in the water. Why were they not cheering?

"It is true we have a plan. And we can speak openly about it now that all of us are named."

No, don't, thought Evan. But at the same time, he listened closely.

"We have used human technology—"

Growls of disapproval cut him off, but Tret only raised his voice.

"—and ingredients we have stolen from humans, to build a device that is powerful enough to kill them all. The scholars are putting the finishing touches on it now!"

There were more growls, but now some of them were approving.

"When the hole is finished, we will drop the bomb on them." Tret growled. "When the hole is finished, we'll pick off their survivors one by one, like Nobs out of a Yellow wall. When the hole is finished, we will be the strongest of dark creatures."

The Wuftoom roared angrily.

"You don't want to hear that you are not the strongest?" Tret mocked. "When will the hole be finished? We are too slow! It is true that we have already drawn good Wuftoom from hunting. It is true that we are all hungry. But what good will our full bellies be if they are pierced like Brode's back with Vitfly claws!"

At this the young ones let out a growl. Evan's body rang with it, but he did not join. What did this mean?

"What should we do?" Tret spread his nubs to take in the waiting clan. "We dig!"

A few more worms joined in the growl this time.

"We dig with everything we have! We dig night and day!"

There were growls and rasps of shock, and more sloshing than before. Evan knew how bad he felt before he went to sleep, when it was approaching daytime.

"Use more Wuftoom, more shifts!" Tret cried. "We will eat less, but we can be done in days, not weeks. We can be rid of our enemy forever!"

There were growls of approval and cries of anger. The room became louder, and Evan wanted to sink into the water. He let himself go a little and tried to put together how he felt. If they attacked sooner, he might not have to help the Vits. His back burned with his hate for them. But what would happen if the Wuftoom lost?

Olen stepped forward from the crowd and stood in the center next to Tret. "I agree that the night's events spell much trouble for our clan. But the Vitflys have attacked isolated hunting groups before. There is no reason to believe that they will come to us sooner than we can go to them."

There were murmurs of approval.

"I ask the young one Tret, how will we dig with less to eat, when the clan is nearly starving now?"

More growls. Evan knew that he had been getting more food than most. Many were lucky to receive one creature every day. From their growls, it was clear that they were stretched to breaking.

"And I answer, the situation is only getting worse!" Tret cried. "Every night there is less food. At this rate, they will starve us before we strike."

Rayden stepped forward from the crowd and stood in the center next to Tret and Olen. He raised his arms high. Even though he was much shorter than both of the others, Evan saw his renowned strength. This was the warrior who had killed and eaten Vitfly.

"This is not an easy night," he said, and the room quieted again to hear his voice. "It is true that Tret and I are often in disagreement. But one thing is clear: It is no coincidence that the Vits have struck our new one Brode. I do not believe they could have done so if they did not have more eyes and ears than we have thought."

Evan froze. Did Rayden suspect?

"I do not know exactly what they know, and this troubles me a great deal. I do not believe that we have time to waste."

The Wuftoom sloshed and eyed each other.

"I call a vote."

At this the cave burst into noise. All around him, the young ones loudly echoed Tret's words. He did not hear the opposing words, but from the noise in the cave, he could tell their views were strong as well.

Evan then knew what he wanted. He wanted the Wuftoom to fight soon. He wanted to fight with them. He wanted to kill and eat every last Vit, so they could never hurt him and they could never hurt his mother. *But we couldn't kill them all,* he thought. Wouldn't the ones that were left take their revenge? He pushed the thought aside. The Wuftoom cared about him. Tret and Suzie had saved his life. He would be dead right now without them.

Evan began to stand, to raise his voice in growling with the young ones, but as soon as he stood fully upright, he fell back into the water. Suzie caught him, and the cave faded to black.

TWENTY-FIVE

*Y*OU SEE, *BRO-DEE.*

Evan awoke. It was nighttime, and the cave was nearly empty. The Wuftoom were working feverishly on Tret's new plan or hunting. Only the scholars had stayed back, twisting all of the clan's membrane into weapons. He had slept for nearly two straight nights and days. He willed his mind to close.

You are a heero now.

Evan thought nothing. He used his mind to push back against Foul. It was easier than it had been with Jordan. The connection to the Vit was weak. For a minute there was silence.

You cannot keep us out for long, Brode.

Again he pushed, and again his mind was silent.

You are still human inside.

He pushed and this time he held on. His body went rigid with the effort, and he stared into the empty water. A minute went by. Two minutes. Ten. He took a long, deep breath.

They will tell Brode all you need to know. Foul's voice was mocking, but it sounded far away.

He breathed out. Silence again. He stood up from his blocks abruptly. It was the first time he had stood by himself since he had been attacked. He held himself in place and focused on the water. His back was sore, but it no longer burned.

I just need more time, he thought. The air inside his brain opened. He could feel the Vitfly, imagine its flapping wings. *I'll get what you need. Just don't hurt her. If you do, I'll never tell you anything. I'll tell everyone you talk to me.*

If you speak a word, she dies.

Evan saw Rayden watching from across the cave. He held a strip of membrane, ready to flip and beat and stretch it into a new kind of rod that he'd invented. Evan nodded a little, but Rayden didn't turn away. Evan's mind was silent again. Foul had made its point. They weren't going away.

He twisted his arms, then slid his legs through the cool sewage. They were stiff at first, but after a few minutes of this the arms twisted firmly and he felt like he could walk. He hoped he would be able to fight.

Rayden was still watching him. Rolling the membrane around his arm, the old one slid across the cave. "Young one, you are not ready to walk," Rayden said gravely. "A Vitfly attack is no small matter. You were cut deeply with both claws and fangs."

"Master Rayden," said Evan. His voice had trouble coming out. His throat was too dry. He bent down and took a drink of water. It took much too long to stand up again.

Rayden continued to regard him gravely.

"Master Rayden, I want to fight. Can you teach me how to use the weapon?" He did not say that he might have to fight sooner than expected. That he might have to beat Vits off his mother rather than tell the Wuftoom's secrets. Rayden would not care about his mother.

Rayden examined Evan, looking him up and down with glowing eyes.

Evan tried not to shake. He had to look like he was strong enough to handle anything. He had to *be* strong enough.

Rayden broke into a wide, thick-fanged grin and clapped Evan on the back. "Standing tall and solid," said Rayden. "That's a Wuftoom!" He sloshed briskly across the cave and returned with one of the weapons. "We call them Feeders," Rayden said, "because they are designed to bring down dinner." The old one's eyes glowed brighter, and he showed a little fang. He held the Feeder out on top of both his nubs. It looked much like a rod, with its bumpy, membrane skin and half a Wuftoom length. But it was thicker on one end. Rayden wrapped both arms around it at the lower end and took a swing. The thick end curved as it slid through the air, and Evan imagined its bend slamming a Vitfly head.

"I designed them myself," said Rayden. "They are membrane filled with flesh. Strong and flexible, like a living Wuftoom!"

Evan pulled back a little. Membrane was one thing, but flesh? How long had its owner been dead for?

Rayden pulled his lips back from his long, thick fangs and laughed. "It is an honor for the dead to be used in this way. There is nothing sacred about our bodies. We don't waste them rotting in the ground."

Like the humans, thought Evan. Inwardly he kicked himself. He had acted human again.

"Let's try it on something real." Rayden nodded toward the place where the targets were hanging.

Evan slowly followed Rayden over. His legs felt like frozen jelly, ready to crack.

The old battered creatures had recently been replaced with fresh skins. Rayden pointed to a Gibben hanging by rope made of its own hair. Because its flesh had been sucked out and eaten, its large eyes took up most of the space on its tiny, shriveled body. In life the Gibben would have been covered in hair, but the Wuftoom had removed that to make the ropes, so it hung naked, staring up at the ceiling and out at Evan all at once. Evan tried not to show the disgust he felt.

"Watch," said Rayden. He showed Evan how to hold the Feeder so that its hump would face the target, and how to twist the weapon just so, to change the way the best part faced. "You can hit anything coming from any direction, if you learn to manipulate the membrane." The Feeder seemed to twist and turn on its own under Rayden's expert nubs. Evan could not even see what the old one was doing to make it turn and flex.

Evan took the Feeder from Rayden.

Rayden gave him another back clap and then went back across the cave to continue making more weapons.

Foul pressed against Evan's mind. He pushed it out, but it came back. He pushed again. Over and over again Foul tried. Evan tried to shut off his thoughts, to focus on nothing but the swing of his Feeder against the targets. He tried to feel how he had moved his membranes to pull himself through the tiny pipes. How they moved separate from his flesh but with it, how they had strength in even tiny movements.

Whack! The Feeder knocked the Gibben off its rope. It went flying into the back wall. As it slid into the water, its giant eyes still stared at Evan. He gripped the Feeder harder and swung again. *Whack! Splash!* An Orpa fell from its string into the water. Evan's arms ached and his head pounded, but he kept whacking with all his strength.

Suddenly, Tret was next to him. "It's time you see what we are doing," Tret said. "I'm told you are feeling better. Master Rayden, is it true?"

Rayden was sitting nearby with the membrane he was working. Evan had not noticed that he'd come back. Now the old leader looked up from his work, taking both Evan and Tret in.

"He is much better," said Rayden. "The Vitflys have gained a formidable enemy." His lips twisted into a smile. Evan was growing to value that smile. There was something precious in it, since it carried the approval of the whole clan.

Evan felt a surge of pride. "Let's go!" he said, smiling bigger than Rayden. He hurt, but he wanted to see the dig.

They slid a little way down the main passage until they reached a fork that went off to the left. It was smaller than the main passage, so that the Wuftoom had to crawl. Evan had seen this passage before and had wondered what was down it.

Before long, they came to a hole in the pipe that did require some smooshing to get through. It opened into a cave in the ground. It was maybe a fifth as large as the main cave, and its floor was dirt rather than water. Several Wuftoom worked, lifting piles of dirt, packing dirt into the walls. In the middle of the cave was a hole. It was several feet wide, with a few blocks piled around it as a warning.

Evan felt it. It went down to where he was supposed to be. To where the air was pure, the dark darker. He looked down on it, leaning over the blocks. Tret put both nubs on Evan's shoulders to hold him back.

"I know," he said. "We'll be there soon, and they'll be the ones hiding."

There were three Wuftoom at the bottom, digging and dropping the dirt onto a platform that looked like a child's sandbox. The platform was hanging from a contraption set up near the edge. It looked as if it was made like the rods, completely out of membrane. Membrane was also plastered down the inside of the hole.

Tret put his nub to his mouth in a shushing motion and walked around the edges of the cave. He examined the walls, sometimes poking at a spot.

"Okay, looks clear," said Tret. "You have to check every time you want to talk. Since it's near our cave, we don't get many of the things we eat hanging around. But you can never be too careful. There are some fools who'd rather take their chances with the Vits." Then he grinned wide. "Their cave is straight beneath us. We got that information from a smarter race. The Gibbens will be glad they sided with us!"

Evan said nothing. He doubted the Gibben whose skin he'd just whacked would have thought so.

"How far down is it?" Evan asked finally. It seemed like

they'd gone down far just to get to the passage they called Yellow, and he knew there were much lower places.

"It's far," said Tret. "But we're combining our human memories with Wuftoom engineering." He plucked at his membrane with another grin. "Some Wuftoom think everything human should be suppressed. But we know how to read. We know how to make things that the humans make. Why shouldn't we use them against the Vits?"

Why shouldn't we care about our mothers? Evan thought. Was it possible that Tret would understand after all?

"Using what we know isn't going to suddenly make us feel human," Tret continued. "It isn't going to make us rush off to be with our human friends. We're still Wuftoom!"

Evan's hope faded. He looked more closely at the membraned hole. The setup really looked like it might work. "And what happens when we get all the way down?"

"We come before the day ends, when most of them will be together. And we drop it! It explodes and spreads poison through their cave." Tret gave his biggest smile of the day. Rasps of approval came from the Wuftoom working nearby.

Evan smiled back, but he found it hard to pay attention. The pressing in his mind grew stronger. He pushed and his head pounded. He was so tired of pushing. He was tired from training all night with the Feeder. He was hungry.

You have been stronger than we thought, Foul hissed, *but we are stronger than you. You will listen to us now.*

Evan froze, his smile plastered to his face.

She hears us in the walls. She cries and cries, the Vit hissed.

He pushed against it, as hard as he ever had before, but he could still feel the presence. He could not think. He could not show them where he was.

"Think you're up for it?" asked Tret. He grinned and nodded toward the hole.

Tell us now and we will let her go.

"Yes," said Evan, too loudly. He tried to keep on smiling. Tret took it for eagerness.

"I knew you'd say that!" Tret clapped him, shoving Evan forward toward the edge, so that he had to throw his nubs over the blocks to keep from falling. Tret grabbed on to his shoulders.

"Sorry, buddy," he said. "Maybe you need a couple more days."

"Yeah, maybe," said Evan. He willed the thoughts out of his mind.

Tell us, Foul hissed.

Evan pushed. How was it still there? He felt a vibration in his mind. Laughter.

Then you will come to us. Tomorrow. Or we come out of the walls to eat her. It laughed a moment longer, and the vibration made Evan stumble into Tret.

Tret's eyes glowed with concern. "Let's get you back."

Evan shook his head. The presence was gone. "I'm fine," he said. "I can start tomorrow."

"I don't think so," said Tret. He kept his nub on Evan's back and guided him up through the hole into the crawler.

Evan's thoughts flooded back in. He couldn't go tomorrow.

He wouldn't do it. The Wuftoom were too close. But the Vits would kill her. Or maybe they wouldn't. Maybe they'd eat her piece by piece. They could hurt her in a million ways. *She would never let anyone hurt me,* he thought. *She'd die first.*

But Tret and the other Wuftoom wouldn't let anyone hurt him either. They cared about him too. He couldn't help the Vits destroy them. Evan moved faster through the crawler, ignoring Tret's protests. He couldn't face Tret anymore, not with what he had to do.

TWENTY-SIX

T HE CAVE WAS STILL AND SILENT. The sentries were facing
   outward toward the passage. Slowly, Evan lifted himself off
of his blocks. He looked carefully around him, but the cave was
filled with sleeping puddles. The day shift would return from
the dig before long. He had to move now.

Cautiously, he began sliding through the water. As he went,
he couldn't help sliding near other Wuftoom. With each tiny
slosh, his heart beat faster. But no one woke.

They sleep so deeply because they have full trust in each oth-
er, Evan thought. *It's in their genes and the way their brains are*
wired. Only my brain didn't get rewired right. They can't count on
me.

He had a sudden urge to wake them, to scream out the truth.
Let them decide what would happen next. But he knew they
didn't care about their mothers. He couldn't take that chance. It
would be his fault, just as if he had killed her himself.

On the far side of the cave from where Evan slept, the scholars slept together. They slept near the products of their labor,
the Feeders and rods and other tools made of the precious
membrane, which were stacked on shelves made of extra sleeping blocks. But Evan was not only going for a weapon to fight

the Vitflys. He would take one, of course. But he also needed something that would hurt a Wuftoom, and there was only one weapon that would do that.

Evan pulled out a Feeder and set it in the water. Carefully, he pulled more of them out and set them softly against the cave wall, until he had created a space large enough for him to push his whole arm through.

He reached through and felt around behind the stack of weapons. For a minute he began to worry. What if Rayden had moved them, afraid of the discord from the lack of food? But no, for one Wuftoom to hurt another was unthinkable. He had not hidden them. Very carefully, so as not to poke himself, Evan slid his nub under a Vit claw. Almost without breathing, he slowly pulled his arm back.

Soon he was staring down at it. This thing that had hurt him so badly that it might have killed him. It was so small, it seemed impossible that it could kill. Yet as he touched it, he felt the moment it had cut into his back and he squirmed, causing the water to ripple around him.

Carefully, he put the claw on top of his Feeder and set about returning the rest of the weapons to their places. All around him, the Wuftoom slept on. Evan returned to the young ones and melted into his blocks to give the appearance of sleep.

Ylander and two other young ones were among the first of the returning shift. As Ylander passed Evan, small gobs of dirt dropped from his arms into the water. They splashed silently but did not fully sink. Someone next to him began to move, then another, until many of the young ones were stirring around him. Only then did he give up his pretense and slowly solidify as well.

From his blocks, he watched as the Wuftoom gathered in the night's groups. The rule was that each group should have three, but now that so many were digging, a few groups had only two. Those groups were the ones with the most experienced Wuftoom, and even then they were assigned only to the water. Tonight Olen and Gorti, another old one, were a group of two.

When they started filing out of the cave, Evan put on his pack, which he had folded his Feeder into, and grabbed his rod. He walked slowly behind the others. As Olen and Gorti reached the exit, Evan came up alongside them.

"Can I join your group?" he asked. The two old ones looked at him gravely.

"It is not safe for you, Brode," said Olen.

"I know everyone thinks that, but I'm not afraid. I'm all healed up. Look." Evan turned his back to the old ones, showing them the twisted membrane. It was knotted and lumpy, but it was no longer open. "I'm sick of being hurt. I don't want to stay here doing nothing."

"We would like you to join us," said Olen, "but Rayden has made it very clear. No one is to allow you to hunt until he gives the word."

"Your desire is admirable. It will not be long now," said Gorti. "There will be no more danger soon." His voice was deep and full of confidence. Evan hoped that it was true.

Olen gave Evan a light clap, and the old ones went on, leaving him at the cave entrance. He wanted to turn to see if Rayden was watching. Could he possibly have noticed that the claw was gone?

Olen and Gorti were hunting for Higgers, and it was a hard assignment. Even during the brief time since Evan and the others had watched Jordan change, the population had decreased. The hunters had to go to another set of big pipes, farther from the main cave than Evan had ever been.

Fortunately, the path was basic. After the dig, he had only one tiny pipe to squeeze through, then a small one that curved around. Then he would be in a pipe that was big enough to crawl in, and he could take that to where Olen was supposed to be going. It was a simple route, yet Evan had had to go over and over it to grasp it.

Everything still looked the same to him. It would be so easy to get lost. And if this simple route was hard, he had no chance of finding his way home.

He set out quickly, not wanting to let anyone stop him. Not willing to think too much, in case he stopped himself. Someone called after him, but he slid faster through the water. He did not turn to see who it had been.

TWENTY-SEVEN

THE TRIP UP THE SMALL PIPE was harder than it had been before. Halfway up, he almost slid backward and had to twist frantically against the pipe. He was stuck for a minute or two before he calmed down enough to go on. But he found the next, slightly larger pipe, squeezed through it, and fell heaving into the crawler.

His pack popped painfully out and he pulled himself onto his nubs with effort. It felt like the pack had ripped the membrane open, and he struggled to calm his breathing down. He listened. All was quiet except for the sound of slowly running water. He turned over on his back and let the water soothe it.

He rolled over onto his stomach, sighing with the coolness of the water, then struggled back to his four nubs. Slowly, he crawled down the pipe, turning his plan over and over in his head. It wasn't much of a plan. He hadn't had time to perfect it. He'd barely even had time to think about it.

"This part's dry, Olen, just like back there." It was Gorti's deep, commanding voice.

"We shouldn't even have bothered here," said Olen. "We'll have to go on outward."

Evan hadn't expected to catch up with them so soon, and

he couldn't stop his nubs' shaking as he came to the end of the crawler and looked down on the large pipe. He took a deep breath. He had to do this.

The old ones were coming from the right. Keeping his head in the pipe's shadow, he watched them slide past. When they were a few Wuftoom lengths past him, he jumped down into the stream.

The old ones whipped around, rods raised. They had taken to carrying packs even in the water now.

"Brode!" exclaimed Gorti. "You nearly got a face full! What were you thinking?"

"What are you doing here?" Olen growled.

Evan panted from exertion. "Master Olen, I'm sorry. I know you told me not to come, but I need to talk to you." His voice sounded as desperate as he was.

The old ones eyed each other. Gorti shrugged.

Olen pursed his lips into a point. "It couldn't wait until later? As a young one, you had fragile health to start with."

"I'm fine," said Evan. "Really, I don't want sit around while the Vits get stronger. I know they hate me most of all."

Olen gave a look to Gorti and sighed. "The Vits hate us all equally," he said. "But I do believe they chose you to attack. It is all the more reason why you should not be here."

"Please, it's important. I need to talk to you alone. You helped me change. I know you're the only one who can help me." It was certainly true.

Gorti shrugged again. "Go on. I will scout the next pipe."

"All right," said Olen. "I will meet you at the next fork." Olen slid toward Evan. His expression was serious, but Evan saw kindness in the glow of his white eyes. Maybe it had been there all along, only as a human, he hadn't wanted to see it.

Evan waited until Olen had lifted himself back into the crawler and followed from behind. Was he really going to do this?

Olen stopped and turned back to Evan. "Do we really need to come this far?" he asked. "Gorti is out of earshot."

"I guess this is far enough," said Evan, glancing behind him. The entrance to the big pipe was nearly gone. There were only a few inches between the top of Olen's body and the pipe.

He jumped onto Olen's back, pushing the old worm forward as he did so. He had to press himself flat against the top of the pipe, squeezing everything but one nub, hoping Olen was squeezed down too much to move. He pressed harder, pulling his head free, so it hung over Olen's head.

"Do you feel that?" he asked. His voice shook and it came out much quieter than he had planned. But fear made his body strong. Olen could say nothing because his head was pinned. "That is a Vitfly claw. It's pressed into your membrane and it will press right through."

Olen struggled beneath him.

Evan pressed down with the claw. Olen's body shook. Evan pressed down harder. Suddenly, Olen pushed up, flattening Evan's head. But Evan kept the claw pressed.

Olen flipped himself over, a simple trick for a Wuftoom, even in a small space. But the Vit claw was in deep, and Evan flipped with him. Even on the bottom, he pressed the claw. Slowly, heaving with effort, he let the claw rip down the old worm's back.

In his pain, Olen wasn't able to hold Evan down, and Evan was able to flip over so that he was on top again. He pulled out the claw and held it to Olen's cheek.

"I'm going home," said Evan. "And you're going to take me there. Or I'll do it again." He rolled backward off Olen and pushed him forward with a kick.

Olen's voice spluttered out of him. He gave half a cry and half a groan and then whirled on Evan. A pinkish pus dripped from his open back. Evan held up the claw.

"*What* are you doing?" Olen shouted. The pipes seemed to vibrate. He sounded more surprised than angry.

Evan's determination faltered. What *was* he doing? "I have to get back home," he said. "I don't know how to get there."

"You could have *asked* me!" Olen shouted.

Evan stared at him.

"*Why* do you want to go home?" Olen said. He was still angry, but he said it a little softer.

Evan gripped the Vit claw tighter. It was too late to lie. "Before I left, the Vits threatened my mother. They said if I didn't come back, they'd eat her."

Now it was Olen's turn to be dumbfounded. Evan watched the shape of his mouth change as he realized the gravity of what Evan had said.

"How much do you remember?" he asked.

"I remember everything," said Evan. "How do you forget your own mother?" The Vit claw began shaking in his hand.

Olen was silent for a second. "It is a long time before we forget," he said. "But a short time before we cease to care. I cannot explain it except that it is in our nature."

"Have you forgotten now?" Evan stared into Olen's eyes. He could not read their glow.

"I have forgotten her name," he said. "I could not tell you what she looked like. But there was a time when I remembered. I even thought of her from time to time."

"But Jordan doesn't remember anything. He was crying for her as he changed, and now he acts like she doesn't even exist."

Olen was silent for another minute, and both Wuftoom shook a little. "You and I were slow to change," said Olen finally. "We are different from the rest." He paused.

Evan tried to process this, but all he could think of was his mother. Where was she now? Where were the Vits?

"Yet I do not think even I would have risked the clan to save her," Olen said.

"I have to save her!" Evan shouted. In his Wuftoom voice, it was a growl. "I don't want to hurt the clan, but I can't let them eat her! Please, Olen, help me!" If he had tear ducts, he would surely have been crying. As it was, his body shook wildly and only a tremendous effort kept him from dropping the Vit claw.

"What do the Vits want you to do?"

"They want me to give them information. To tell them how

to get into the Wuftoom cave. I'm not going to tell them. I don't even know. But they told me I had to come now. They won't wait any longer."

"How did they tell you?" Olen's voice was calm now, but his eyes never left Evan's.

"They've been talking to me in my head."

Olen sucked his lips until they were only a tiny speck. "Either you are truly different or the Vits are much stronger than we thought."

"It's me," said Evan. "I'm sure of it. They can't talk to me for long. Just long enough to tell me they'll kill her if I don't come! Please, you have to show me the way!" Evan's shaking nub held the Vit claw up.

"Put that away," said Olen. "You are a Wuftoom. What matters to you matters to me." Both worms stood silent. "I said, *put it away.* I am going to help you." Olen's eyes now glowed with anger, but Evan saw that he meant what he said.

With shaking arms, he lowered the claw. The space was too tight for him to put it in his pack. He sank back onto his legs.

"I should gather an assault force," said Olen. "Yet I fear you were right to keep your secret. There are many who would not understand that you are as much Wuftoom as they. There are many who would counsel against helping you."

"We don't have time!" cried Evan, his face now turned down. He did not want to look at Olen, whose pus was still dripping into the water. "I have to go tonight."

"Then we will go now." Olen sucked in a breath of pain,

which he quickly tried to cover, and started sloshing down the pipe. As he crawled, he rolled back and forth, flushing the cool water over his cuts.

"I'm sorry," Evan said. "I didn't know you would help me. I thought you would try to stop me and let her die."

"There are many who would have," said Olen. "I did not treat you well when you were a proem. You had every reason to believe that I would do the same."

Evan did not know what to say. It was true, and yet he had been wrong.

"It is in our nature to hate humans," Olen continued. "They are a danger. It is difficult to like a proem, when he hates us just as much. But that does not excuse me. I of all Wuftoom should have realized you might remember." They went on in silence, with Olen stopping to flush his back every few feet.

After a while Olen stopped in front of a small pipe that they would have to slide up.

"I can't carry my pack with this," he said, pointing a nub at his hurt back.

"You can have mine when we get there," said Evan. "I can't shoot anyway."

Olen took his pack all the way off and dropped it in the putrid water. Evan watched more pink pus drip over his back. Almost imperceptibly, the old worm's body shook.

"Follow me, Brode," he said quietly. "I will lead you where you need to go." Olen shoved his head into the hole, and in a flash, the rest of him was gone. Evan jumped in after him, following the old one's wake.

TWENTY-EIGHT

OLEN SPLASHED HARD into a main pipe, falling head-first without catching himself. He sprawled in the water and gasped for breath. Evan, too, came headfirst, but he caught himself with his nubs and was soon upright, clutching his claw. As soon as his pack expanded, he quickly put it away inside. Hurriedly, he glanced up and down the pipe. It was all clear.

Olen struggled but pulled himself upright. He looked terrible. Pus was still oozing from his open back despite his dump into the water. Evan had not meant to hurt him so badly, only to scare him. He wanted to cry out how sorry he felt, but Olen had already turned and was slowly sloshing upstream.

Evan tried to remember. He thought he recognized this tube. He thought it was the one leading to the pipes that led up to his bedroom, but he couldn't be sure because it looked almost exactly like the one leading to the Wuftoom cave. But he knew they hadn't gone back there. This was in the complete opposite direction, and it was far enough away to be the right place. His breathing quickened, pulsing his whole body in and out.

After a while Olen stopped at the entrance to a smaller pipe. Evan had to step backward to keep from getting dripped on by his pus.

"This is the one," said Olen.

"Aren't you coming with me?" Evan asked.

"First you must tell me what you plan for us to do."

"I brought one of the Feeders," said Evan.

"And what do you expect to do with that?"

"I don't know." His planning hadn't come that far. "I thought I might lie to them. Tell them there's a way in. Anything to make them go away."

Olen shook his head gravely. "The lie will last until they reach your mind. You will only buy yourself a little time."

"But it might be enough," said Evan. "We might destroy them!"

Olen nodded. "Tell them we are digging a hole into their home."

Evan gaped at him.

Olen's mouth twisted into a tiny smile. "Only tell them the wrong location. If you are careful, the half truth of it will keep them from pulling the whole truth out of your mind."

Now Evan nodded. He could do that. They would not hear anything from him that he did not want to tell.

Olen saw the determination on Evan's face. "I will take the weapons, the rod and the Feeder. I will stay out of sight. If you need me, I will be there."

"Are you sure you can fight?" Olen's open wound showed no sign of closing, and he still shook a little as they talked.

"I am old," he said. "I have been hurt more and endured longer."

Evan hesitated. He was not ready. Olen saw Evan's fear, but

he did not wait. He pushed his arms and head into the tiny pipe. They squooshed and Olen's legs twisted. He was having trouble pulling himself in. Evan pushed his legs softly, and they slid in farther. Evan had no choice now but to follow. Slowly, the two Wuftoom slid upward. Evan had to use his strength to keep the old one going, but too quickly they rose above the ground.

It was easy to tell where the surface was. Though they were still in the pipes, something about the air had changed. The pipes felt thinner and more fragile. It was harder to trust that they would hold him in. Olen pushed into a fork on their left side. Evan's body wanted to expand against the pipes, but they held him. He burst out into the smoothness of the bathtub and gripped on to it, pulling with both his arms and legs.

Olen expanded more slowly than he should have. His body fell against Evan's, and Evan had to push the old one up. Olen's body heaved in pain, but he climbed out of the bathtub.

Evan could not imagine dealing with the Vit wound while being so far above the ground. What had he done? But he did not have time to think about it. Olen held out his nub. Evan pulled off his pack and pulled the Feeder out of it. He fixed the pack to Olen's back and handed him both weapons. Olen put the rod to the pack and Evan heard the water being sucked in.

Evan also heard something else. The rapid flapping of many wings. Evan froze and his eyes met Olen's. Olen nodded. Evan moved slowly forward. He felt that he was not in control of his body, as if a puppeteer had taken over to push him through these suicidal steps. The door to the bedroom was slightly ajar. Olen slid behind it and nodded again. Evan reached his nub into the space and pulled the door open.

The room was full of Vitflys.

They saw him at once. At least twenty hairy Vitfly faces, fangs hanging sharp, turned toward him. The sound of flapping filled his flesh. His mother sat on the bed. Her back was against the wall and her knees were pulled into her chest. She stared straight ahead of her, unseeing. Evan clenched his nubs, but there were no weapons in them.

"Okay, I'm here," he said. He wanted to yell it, but it was almost a whisper that came out.

"Proem," Foul hissed. It flapped forward from the pack. The rest flapped their wings in place, boring holes in him with their glowing eyes. All the Vitflys would have looked the same to Evan before he had changed, but he could tell the difference between them now. He recognized Foul's hairy face, its sharp, mean fangs.

"It's Evan," said Evan.

At this his mother suddenly looked up and around her. Her eyes were strangely vacant and she still didn't see him. It was so dark, it would have been hard for a human to see.

"Mom!" he cried.

Then she saw him, or at least knew he was there.

Evan ran to her, pushing through the Vitflys, who lazily parted to let him pass.

Tears streamed down his mother's face.

"Don't cry. I'm fine. I still look terrible, but I'm fine." He wasn't at all fine, but he willed himself to ignore the rising panic. "What have they done to you? Did they hurt you?"

She looked up and around again vacantly, as if she couldn't quite see them. She shook her head.

"What have you done to her?" Evan whispered. He had trouble making himself talk. He would have been crying too if it were possible with Wuftoom eyes. Foul had followed him and now hovered next to his head.

"We have done nothing yet, *Evan*," the creature hissed. "She is lucky you got here when you did. My kin were anxious for their first taste of human flesh." Evan glanced quickly at his mother, but she seemed not to have heard or understood.

"Well, send them away. I have what you want," Evan said.

Foul turned and screeched at the other Vitflys. It sounded awful, nothing like words. But somehow the creatures understood. One by one, they flew up to the light fixture. The flapping of their wings and the suction noises as they left made Evan feel even more sick. Five of them remained, still flapping. Now all turned to watch Evan and Foul.

"Well?" Foul hissed.

Without thinking, Evan almost glanced toward Olen, but he caught himself. His mother's hand clutched his and squeezed, though her eyes still stared vacantly ahead.

"Mom?" he said to her, ignoring the Vitfly. "Mom? Stay with me. They're all going to go away soon. You'll never have to see them again."

Her eyes flitted toward him. Her hair was disheveled and she was wearing her ratty old flannel nightgown, the same one she had worn almost every night. At once he felt a wave of guilt. She was so poor only because of him. Only because he'd weighed her down. Not just these past two years but his whole life. Again, she only nodded and looked away.

"You've done something to her," he said. "You've already hurt her. Why should I tell you anything now?"

Foul flapped, and so did the other five behind it. Foul's eyes glowed and its fangs hung sharply. It gave a long, slow hiss. Evan knew just what it meant. He knew that they could do worse to her. At least she was still alive. Maybe she could be helped.

"They're digging a hole," he said. "I'll show you." He walked to his shelves, which were exactly as he had left them. There was a book of drawing paper. He opened it, wrapped his nub around a pencil, and began to awkwardly draw the Wuftoom cave. He had no doubt the Vitflys knew where that was. Then he drew the nearby passages. Where the real hole was, he drew only the pipe.

As he drew, he felt something intrude on him. He looked up into Foul's glowing eyes. There was no indication of how it was doing it, but it was indeed Foul. As their eyes met, the feeling became stronger. He continued to draw. Several passages down and farther from the main cave, he drew an X.

"This is where they're digging," he said. To avoid thinking, he kept talking. "They plan to dig down to your level and then catch you by surprise. A spider told them that you take this passage every night." It was partly true. The passage Evan had marked was part of the Gibbens' information.

"How many will be there?" Foul hissed.

"Many," said Evan. "I don't know exactly, but enough so they think they can get you all."

A strange sound came from the Vits. An uneven kind of hiss. Laughter?

"So now you know. Leave me and my mom alone." He turned to face her, waiting to hear them leave.

"You have done us a great service, Evan," Foul said. "As a test case, I must say you came out extremely well."

Evan squeezed his mother's hand harder, willing himself to ignore it, to just wait until they were all gone.

"It appears the mental transformation was completely blocked."

Evan turned to look at it. "You mean, you purposely kept me from changing?" As he held his mother's hand, he didn't know whether to be angry or grateful. They had done it to destroy the Wuftoom, but what would he be if he had forgotten her?

Foul chuckled its mottled hiss. The other five remaining Vits moved closer. The air from their wings fluttered across his face. "But you have a Wuftoom's tasty flesh."

Evan's blood froze. He gripped his mother's hand and arm. She was crying now, still lost in her own place.

"You said I would be free. I've done what you asked."

A heavy spray of water hit Evan's face. The Vits screeched. Evan's mother sat up. She grasped on to his nubs.

"Evan?"

"It's okay, it's okay," he said. Another spray of water came, hitting the bed in front of them. "It's just water. It's okay."

There was more screeching, then the crunch of a Feeder meeting a Vit body. The Vits surrounded Olen. He had given up loading the water and was now beating the Vits with the weapons in both arms. Three Vits lay on the ground.

Evan looked around for something to grab, but he saw nothing. He jumped off the bed and picked up a dead Vit. With all his strength, he threw it at one of the three attacking Olen. It missed, but the live Vit was forced to dodge.

Olen tossed Evan the Feeder, and Evan struck. This time the blow connected. The Vit fell to the ground in front of him. Another one landed on Olen's back. Its claws dug in, right where Evan had clawed him. Olen grunted and swung at the last one, Foul, who deftly dodged. Evan beat at Olen's back. The Vit jumped free and, with a hiss, disappeared into the fixture. Only Foul was left.

Olen and Evan faced it, arms raised to swing.

"Olen," Foul hissed.

Olen screeched Foul's Vitfly name, baring his fangs.

"I hope you live, old worm," Foul screeched. It barely sounded like words. "So you can see how we destroy you." With a loud flapping, it flew up into the ceiling.

Olen fell to the floor. His wound was now a gaping hole. Pink and yellow juice flowed freely onto the rug.

"Mom!" cried Evan.

She was sitting straight up on the bed, alert, watching them. Tears streamed down her face.

"Mom, you have to leave! Go anywhere, I don't care. You can't stay here. They'll come back."

She grasped both of his arms, then put her arms around him. She was shaking with her tears.

"I'll come back," he whispered. "Leave me a note. Behind the painting, where they won't see it. I'll find you." He pulled himself away and ran to Olen. Olen's body was heaving, but his eyes were vacant. Evan grabbed his legs and dragged him backward through the bathroom.

"I love you," his mother said. "Never forget that."

"I love you, too," he said. "I will be back." He pulled Olen into the bathtub. He had never moved an unconscious worm before and he was not sure it would work, but he held Olen's legs together with his own nubs and began sliding into the drain. Olen's body compressed as Evan pulled it with him.

He had left the weapons and the pack, but still the trip was difficult and strange. Olen's useless membranes did not grab, and the progress was breathtakingly slow. By the time they fell together into the large pipe, it seemed like an impossible amount of time had passed. As Olen expanded, he let out a groan.

"Olen!" Evan cried. "You're alive!"

Olen's eyes scanned the pipe above him. Evan held his head up just above the water.

"Once," said Olen, his voice raspy and soft, "I looked up and saw the sky."

"You remember that?" Evan whispered. He knew some worms remembered, but did they *remember?*

"Those who do not remember believe that memory brings only sadness. Confusion and disloyalty." Olen coughed, and a yellow liquid sputtered from his mouth.

"Don't try to talk," said Evan. He lowered Olen more, so as much of the cool water covered him as possible.

"But *we* know, there can be nothing lost by knowing, and thinking and *being* more." Olen's eyes glowed, then flickered, then glowed again.

"Master Olen, please," said Evan. "I'm going to take you back. You'll be all right. I'm so sorry."

"I am sorry, young one. I cannot help you now." Olen raised a nub as if to grab Evan's arm. But the arm fell back into the water, and the worm's eyes flickered out.

"Olen!" The body did not move. Evan shook, holding on to him, still holding his head above the water. A Higger darted past him and swam quickly beyond his reach.

TWENTY-NINE

EVAN'S MIND RACED and his body ached. He had hated and feared Olen, even after he had changed. He had never talked to him, never asked him about his life. In his hundreds of years as a Wuftoom, Olen must have known a great deal. If he could remember life as a human so long ago, what strange and amazing stories could he have told? But Evan had never asked him. He had been so worried about himself, so focused on the bad things. Why couldn't he have just *asked?*

Olen's body dragged behind him in the water. It no longer held its shape and was loose and liquid. Were it not for the membranes, it would have drifted into the water and mixed until it was all gone. What would Olen tell him to do? He had come with Evan alone out of fear for what the others would do if they knew the truth. But hiding it had gotten Olen killed. Would any of the others understand?

The night was drawing to a close. Most Wuftoom were back inside the cave. Some were already arranging their sleeping blocks.

Evan made himself go in, sliding Olen's body through the water. Tret and Rayden were together, in the center where Rayden and his group sat. Evan headed toward them. Growls rose up around him as he passed some Wuftoom, but he did not answer them. As they saw what he dragged, they began to crowd around him, so that when he reached the center, he was in a group of growling voices, bodies pressing into each other, water sloshing high around him.

Tret and Rayden watched him approach. Their eyes glowed strong, but Evan was not sure what it meant, the way their lips twisted around themselves. Evan sank into the water and pulled Olen's body forward.

"I'm sorry," he said. Rayden grabbed on to Olen and let out a short cry. Then Evan saw that Olen's hunting partner, Gorti, was with them, and Gorti, too, let out a cry and grasped the unformed membrane. Tret pushed past Rayden and wrapped his nub around Evan's back, but instead of clapping him, he let the nub rest and pulled Evan closer.

"What happened, Brode?" he asked softly.

Evan's eyes fell on Rayden and Gorti, who were rolling Olen's body, folding and shaping it in a way Evan had never seen before. It was clear this was a ritual, a way of honoring the dead. The other worms had fallen silent, and he felt the glow of all their eyes, pushing past him to watch the act. Tret, too, fell silent, and together they watched as Rayden and Gorti molded Olen's body into a square.

The arms and legs of membrane hung loose from the thickness of the liquid body, and Rayden carefully tied all four empty limbs into a knot that rested in a crown above the body. They had forced liquid back into the head, so that Olen's face was recognizable, but it was not quite shaped right. Evan had to force himself to look at it. Olen had died protecting him, had understood him when no one else had. Everyone should know how brave he was.

"He saved me and my mother from the Vitflys," Evan said. Tret's grip tightened around his back. He felt Gorti's and Rayden's eyes on him. Olen's eyes were sunk into the re-formed head, well out of sight. Evan took a breath in.

"I know I'm not supposed to care, but I do. They threatened to kill her if I didn't help them. I was afraid to tell anyone. I was afraid you wouldn't let me go. I threatened Master Olen with a Vit claw to try to force him to show me the way home." They didn't need to know he'd actually cut him. Evan looked away from the body as he left this important part out.

"Master Olen said he understood. He said I can be a Wuftoom and still remember. He said he would help me. He told me to tell the Vits about the hole but give them the wrong location. So I did that. But they wouldn't let me go like they promised. They were going to eat me. So Master Olen fought them. I tried to bring him back, but he had so many cuts."

A hundred pairs of eyes glowed.

Some growled in anger and others in sympathy or sadness, so that a wild disorder filled the cave. Rayden's group held the mass back, while he and Tret peppered Evan with questions. Evan explained how the Vits had talked to him in his head, how it had felt and sounded, and most of what he had done.

"Brode," said Rayden, when he had heard the whole story

and all its details three times, "I fear I have done you a great disservice. I was blinded by belief in our own strength, and I could not see what they had done to you." He paused for a long minute, his mouth a straight and solemn line. Then he nodded at Tret. "Tret, it is even more clear to me that your plan to speed up our attack is sound."

Tret's lips twisted in silence. "You should have come to me," he said. "Why didn't you come to me?"

Evan could not meet his burning eyes. "I was afraid you'd let her die." He looked down into the water.

Tret said nothing else, but his eyes went on glowing with an intense light.

"Brode," said Rayden. His voice was not harsh, but his eyes glowed hard and steady. "If you so much as feel a tingle of awareness in the farthest reaches of your mind, you will inform Tret at once."

Evan nodded, still looking down. The crowd slowly calmed and went on with the work of arranging the blocks for the day that was now breaking. Evan could do nothing but head to the young ones' place with Tret.

"What will happen to Olen?" Evan asked. The old ones had moved the body to their place on the far side of the cave.

"The old ones will take him in secret and separate his body from his membrane. His membrane and his flesh will become weapons that we will use to beat the Vits to pieces." Tret let out a breath. "Brode," he continued. "I am not angry at you. I am angry at these creatures. This enemy so strong that they can invade our minds at birth and stunt us into half-human, half-Wuftoom things."

Ylander and Suzie had come to meet them, and both heard this last statement. They had both heard the story as it made its way around the cave.

"Master Olen thought Brode was a Wuftoom," said Suzie. "Or he would never have helped him." She put her nub around Evan and gave him a soft pat. He could not look at her.

"Slow Change Olen," said Tret. Without looking back at them, he sloshed to his blocks, tossing unartful sprays behind him.

"Brode, don't pay attention to him," said Suzie. "His feelings are hurt because he was the last to know. We all know why you didn't tell us."

Ylander nodded with her.

"Do you really think I'm a Wuftoom?" Evan asked, now looking at them. Their eyes glowed with a normal tint. They looked just as they had before.

Suzie rubbed a nub over his bald head. "You didn't tell the Vits the truth, did you?"

Evan shook his head.

"A human would have done that. A human would have hated us. It's in our nature to hate each other."

"I don't hate humans," said Evan, looking down again.

"Look at us," said Ylander. "You don't hate us, do you?"

Evan shook his head again.

"Then you are one of us." Ylander looked at Suzie and

twisted his lips into a sort of smile. "It's Tret who insists we should use what we learned as humans. That's how he got the scholars to make the bomb. It's a funny time to decide that forgetting is better."

"Tret hasn't forgotten," said Suzie. "He just needs a little time."

"Attention, Wuftoom!" Rayden was standing in the middle of the cave, arms raised. "You have all heard about the heroic death of Master Olen."

The Wuftoom were silent and still.

"He died protecting the young one Brode, and with him the entire clan. He died at the claws of—" Rayden screeched. It was Foul's name, loud and clear and awful.

The Wuftoom broke into an uproar. Screeches of Foul's name combined with growling and cries of anguish.

"Now they know we have a plan. They do not know the whole truth, but we must not give them time to learn. There is no more time! We attack before the next night falls!"

THIRTY

RAYDEN WOKE THE WUFTOOM well before the day was gone.

Tret gave the assignments to the young ones. "Ylander, Suzie." Tret glared at Evan, white eyes glowing. "And Brode. Rayden has decided that all those who have fought Vitflys will be present when we drop the bomb. You will be with us at the dig. Should any manage to make it up after the bomb, we will fight them. Otherwise, we will strike those that escape the lower teams. Rutgi." Tret nodded to Jordan.

Jordan clenched his nub around his rod, and his eyes burst into a bright glow. "You will go with a team led by Blottix," Tret continued. "You will be down in the tunnels nearest the Vit home, waiting to catch those that escape from the blast. You will kill all that you find." Tret had not needed to add that last part, but clearly it pleased him to say it. His eyes now glowed like Jordan's. "We'll kill every last one." Tret splashed off toward Blottix, who was a few yards away.

Evan looked down until he was sure Tret was gone.

Suzie patted him lightly on the back.

"Brode!" Jordan exclaimed. "I almost wish I'd been clawed, so I could be there at the dig!"

Evan twisted his lips in an attempt to smile. "You'll get to fight plenty," he said. "You'll get to beat them to death with your own arms. That's better than watching a bomb drop." He imagined beating Foul with his Feeder. How it would sound when the membrane connected with the Vitfly's fangs.

"I'm going to get more than anyone!" Jordan said.

Evan cringed at his excitement. The image of his revenge on Foul faded. Did Jordan really understand the danger? He had never even seen a Vit alive. Jordan and everyone else could end up empty membrane.

"Be careful," Evan said.

"My team here!" yelled Blottix.

"Don't worry, Brode," said Jordan. "We're going to destroy them. Then it'll be a feast!" Jordan turned away as he said it, as his group was already starting to move. His fangs shone, and his smooth shoulders rippled as his pack adjusted for the walk.

The mention of food made Evan's body tremble. He knew all the other Wuftoom felt the same. No Wuftoom had received a full meal since the naming, and growling matches erupted daily. All were desperate for this night to end, and with a feast of Vitfly.

Tret's group began to form around where Evan stood. It was fairly small, only about fifteen, since only those who would assist in the bomb dropping were truly needed. The rest were honoraries who'd fought the Vitflys, like Evan.

The main force gathered around Rayden, and Evan saw them raise their weapons in unison as Rayden performed a final drill. Evan was in awe of the old ones, who twisted their rods so expertly that they seemed to move faster than the water shot. Master Gorti was one of the best. He saw Evan watching and nodded.

Evan nodded back. He wanted to tell Gorti he was sorry again, that he'd do anything to have Olen back. But there was no time. There was no time for anything.

Tret was convinced his bomb would work, that those near the Wuftoom cave would have nothing to do. But a wary feeling nagged at Evan, and he gripped his weapon tightly as Tret talked.

" . . . the force of the explosion will break the remaining barrier between the dig and the Vit home. The poison will fall into their cave and spread out. The barrier is uneven because of the rush, so I'm going to go down into the hole and set the bomb at the best spot. Ylander will hoist me back up. Ylander and Suzie will guard the dig in the unlikely event that somehow a Vit gets up through the poison. The rest of us will return to the main group. Any questions?"

There were low growls of assent.

Tret turned toward Rayden's group and held up a nub. Rayden held up his nub and rolled it down. The Wuftoom growled, and Evan joined in. His voice rippled and grew louder with the voices of the others, until the cave was filled with a rough song. They never practiced sounds like this, yet it came together. Now Evan thought it was beautiful.

The music of the growling slowly fell, and Tret turned toward the exit, the group following behind. Ylander and Suzie joined Tret at the front, and they slid strongly through the water.

Evan lagged behind a little. Their steps were filled with a purpose and a confidence he did not feel. Of course he had not told the Vits about the bomb, but weren't they smart enough to guess? Wouldn't they have defenses the Wuftoom didn't know about?

They packed into the cave. Evan had no part in the bomb dropping, so he worked his way to the back. Suzie was helping strap Tret into the harness that would lower him down into the pit. Ylander was testing the pulley system.

All the Wuftoom had weapons in both nubs and packs on their backs. Despite expecting no trouble, they had come prepared. Evan suspected that some hoped for trouble so they would get a chance to take out an enemy and eat it. Even though he knew it was foolish, Evan could not help but feel the same wish. He had never for an instant forgotten the taste of Vitfly blood. His fluids pumped through his body.

Suzie checked Tret's straps one final time, smoothing them carefully under her nub. She said something to Tret, but Evan couldn't hear it. Tret nodded and said something back. He walked toward the edge of the hole. Ylander held on to the end of the holster, which was a membrane rope that ended in a coil on the ground beneath them.

All the Wuftoom squeezed forward to see, and Evan pressed up against the back of them. He saw Suzie and Tret pressed together, Suzie handing Tret a dark, round object, Tret holding it reverently. A cheer rose from the crowd. Tret turned and raised the bomb high in the air. His face was obscured by the Wuftoom raising their nubs with him.

Then Tret was gone, Ylander was pulling, the crowd was cheering. Noise came from the hole below. The crowd kept cheering at first. Then Tret flew back up the hole. Ylander grasped for the pulley, but it was no longer tight. Tret hit the cave floor and rolled out of Evan's sight.

Evan heard a whirring noise, then the sucking sound of loading rods. He had just enough time to raise his Feeder before a dark, flapping, screeching cloud of Vitflys poured out of the hole.

THIRTY-ONE

BLASTS OF WATER filled the cave, and the Vits screeched and dived around them. Vits cracked against Feeders, and Wuftoom rasped in pain as Vit claws dug into their flesh.

Evan dropped his rod and ducked to the ground, Feeder still up. It was the defensive posture that Rayden had taught. Prepare to roll and beat, the war hero had said. Some others were also on the ground, but many were still standing, still trying to spray. A few Vits were sent up or backward, but they had the advantage. There were too many of them.

How did they know? Evan thought. A sick feeling spread through his body. A Vit dived for him and he smashed it, rolled to his right, smashed it again. Another dived and this time he just rolled until he was stopped by hitting something soft.

It was a motionless Wuftoom. A Vit sat on top of him, its fangs dug deep into his flesh.

Evan stifled a scream and rolled back the other way. He heard a loud pop, and water spewed over his back. A Vit must have burst his pack.

He dropped his feeder, rolled over onto his stomach and lay still. The flaps of his burst pack felt sticky on his membrane. The air was filled with screeching, yet the sounds stayed above him. Amid what sounded like wild chatter were the fluctuations of Vit language. Evan willed his body not to beat, not to pulse in and out with breath so that the Vits would notice he was alive.

A warbled screech came from across the cave. Evan heard the flapping of their wings change and the air swirl as the Vits retreated. Then came the familiar sucking sound, like when they went up the light fixture, but stronger. He waited and heard nothing and waited more. Slowly, he rolled onto his back and rose.

The room was filled with bodies. Some were deflated and half eaten, but others were whole. Evan almost called out but stopped himself for fear the Vits would hear him. Instead, he walked through the room, shaking each body to see if the Wuftoom was alive. The first two did not move, and the third one was nearly eaten through, but the fourth one he touched groaned.

It was Ylander. His back was badly cut, and Evan had to roll him over and prop him up. He looked dazed.

"They're gone," Evan whispered. "You're the first I've found alive."

Ylander's eyes flickered weakly.

Evan dragged him backward and propped him against the wall, going on with his search. He found one more alive, a middle-aged Wuftoom named Horg. He had an old Vit scar under his mouth that had always made him look grizzled and strong. But now it combined with the claw marks on his head to make him look aged and weak. Evan pulled Horg to the wall with Ylander.

Finally, Evan came to the upper left corner of the cave. There were three Wuftoom there, one lying face-up. Evan did not recognize him. His features had sunk away and not much of his body was left. The other two were face-down. One appeared to be reaching for the other. His nubs were stretched out and lying on top of the other one's back. Evan shook him and his arms came free.

Evan didn't recognize him, either.

His front side was covered in Vit holes. If he had moved after being clawed like this, Evan could not imagine how he had done it. There was almost no membrane on his stomach and some of his belly was just gone, yet somehow he had retained his shape. Then Evan saw what he had been reaching for. Tret's body was strangely lifted, as if he was lying on top of something. He still had the bomb.

Evan stood for a few seconds, knowing what he had to do but unable to do it. He stared down at Tret's back. The knot was gone now. It had been torn apart so well, it looked like pus covered in tiny squares of plastic wrap. He reached down a nub to roll Tret off his precious package. Tret coughed.

"Tret!" Evan dropped to his knees, or where his worm legs folded. "Tret, can you hear me?" Slowly, he tried to grab Tret from underneath, where it wouldn't hurt so much, and rolled him off the bomb, onto his back. His front side was untouched.

"Drop it," Tret whispered. His voice barely carried from his mouth, but Evan understood.

He picked up the bomb. It was a sphere made of some kind of creature skin, and heavy.

"What do I do?" he asked. It looked as harmless as one of their dead targets.

"Pull . . ." Tret gasped.

Evan turned the thing around. Then he saw what Tret must mean. There was a knot in the skin.

"This?" he asked, holding the knot up to Tret's face.

Tret gave a little nod. His eyes glowed as fiery as Evan had ever seen them.

Evan nodded back. He pushed past two bodies and stood over the dig. He wrapped his nub around the knot and pulled. The knot came out of the sphere, along with an uneven patch of skin. He dropped it into the hole. He listened, expecting a loud explosion, but he heard only a tiny pop. He couldn't tell what was going on down at the bottom. But Tret smiled. It was the first time Tret had smiled at him since Evan had come back with Olen. His fangs almost seemed to glow.

"Got . . . them," he said.

But Evan wondered how many of them were still down there. Had they got any at all? "Tret." He got back down on the floor and grabbed Tret's arm. "I'm going back to get some help for you. Will you be all right?"

"Are you" — he coughed a little — "the only one . . ."

"No, there are two others. Ylander and Horg. But they're badly hurt." He pointed to where the young one and the middle-aged worm were sitting. Neither one appeared aware of what was going on.

"Suzie . . ." Tret pressed his lips together and his eyes flickered.

Evan looked around him. He had touched every body, yet he had not recognized his friend. "I didn't see her. She might have been . . ." He pressed his lips together too. Tret could finish that sentence for himself. She might be so eaten that she couldn't be recognized.

"Brode," Tret whispered. Even with his super hearing, Evan had to lean in close. "They will be back to eat us. There's no telling what you'll find when you go back. You have to move us into the pipes now."

Evan realized the truth of it. The Vits would not leave good food lying here for long.

"The smaller the better," Tret whispered. "We will lose less flesh compressed." And the Vitflys could never compress tight enough to get them. Evan nodded.

It was slow and awkward work, but Evan managed to smoosh Horg through the little entrance pipe and into the crawler and then to force him up the first small pipe he came to. He then came back for Ylander, who was now a little more coherent.

"How did they know?" he whispered.

Evan choked back a breath. "I don't know!" He could not hide his distress.

"They're stronger than we ever realized," said Ylander.

Evan pushed him into the crawler and set about dragging him toward the pipe where he had left Horg. "I thought I would put you all together," he said. "Do you think that's best?"

Ylander coughed and nodded. "Better together."

"I'll be back for you as soon as I can. As soon as it's safe."

Ylander nodded again, but his eyes were growing dim. Evan

shoved him into the pipe and made sure all of him was pressed into its depths before returning for Tret.

How *did* they know? Maybe they had just figured it out. They just hadn't trusted him and had looked for another place. Or maybe they had bribed some nosy creature to tell them the truth. But Evan didn't believe these explanations. He knew they'd gotten the information from his mind somehow.

Tret was sitting up a little, but he didn't look good. His eyes were faint and his pus dripped onto the floor. Evan lifted him up and pulled him slowly toward the pipe. Tret tried to assist, but he had very little strength.

"What if they got it from my mind?" Evan asked. He hadn't meant to, but he couldn't keep the thought in.

"You didn't mean to give it to them," Tret said.

"I shouldn't stay with you," said Evan. "You can't tell me anything without them knowing."

"Brode," said Tret weakly, "we do not leave our own behind."

I'm still not one of you, Evan thought as he thrust Tret into the pipe, but he said nothing. He dragged Tret through the water, and the young leader moaned a little as the cooling water hit his injured back.

"I'll tell everyone I see," said Evan as he stopped in front of the small pipe. "You won't have to rely on me. Someone will come back for you."

Tret's eyes were steady and he looked up at Evan, his body half sunk into the water. Evan held on to his nubs.

"I know you'll come back if you can," said Tret.

"I will!" Evan cried, and it sounded too loud in the silence.

But he meant it. Somehow this was his fault, and he wasn't going to let his friends die. Tret gasped as Evan lifted him up and directed his nubs into the hole.

"I'm going to grab on to your legs and push," said Evan. "You'll feel the others."

"Good luck, Brode," said Tret. Evan could not tell if it was said with full goodwill, but it was not said with anger.

"I'll come back," he said, and pushed Tret in. He stood there for a second, taking in the sound of the slowly running water. Then he went back for a weapon.

The cave was still and deadly silent. Evan tried not to look at them, what was left of his new friends. But he could not close his eyes and he could not look away while also looking for a weapon. They were all losing their shape. Those with the worst wounds had spilled out onto the dirt of the cave floor, where their insides pooled in puddles of sticky goo. Evan recognized it too well. A sickness welled inside of him that did not fit in his Wuftoom body.

He did not bother looking for a pack and rod, since he still wasn't a good shot. He would be better off with just a Feeder. It was all the better, since the packs were well attached to his dead friends.

A Feeder lay next to a half-formed Wuftoom. He reached down for it and pulled. As he did so, the body sighed a little. Evan started with hope but quickly realized it had just let out a little air and some more goo. The tip of the Feeder had been stuck a little under the body. He tried to make himself stay calm.

It was then that he realized it was Suzie. She was face-down and half of her was gone, but somehow he knew. Not long ago, he couldn't have imagined how he could tell this worm apart from any other. They all looked exactly the same, even in life. He reached down and gently lifted the body. Her face was mis-shapen, but it was her. It was the distance between the eyes, the point of the fangs. He turned his head away.

Suzie had been nicer to him than anyone. And she was so young. Evan started shaking. He set Suzie gently down, gripped the Feeder, and ran to the hole in the pipe, pulling himself back in so quickly that he stumbled and fell on his face in the crawler. The cool water did nothing to soothe him.

Still shaking, he listened. There was some noise, but it was far away. He would have to head toward it. But what was it? How many were there? All the fear that he had blocked out came rushing in, all the violence. The wings flapping, the fangs tearing, the slurping of flesh. He dropped his Feeder into the stream and lay in the water, shaking.

The walls of the crawler seemed to close in around him. He thought he could smell something. Something sweet and awful. He knew he couldn't smell it, yet it was there.

The noise from down the pipes suddenly grew louder. He jumped, and his head squooshed against the pipe. *I promised I would get help,* he thought. *I'm going to do it.* He pulled the weapon out of the water and, still shaking a little, he slowly began to crawl.

THIRTY-TWO

H E HUNG BACK in the crawler that emptied into the main pipe. The Wuftoom were in the water and the Vits were in the air. But it wasn't the carnage of before. These Wuftoom were outnumbered, but not half so badly. They were well armed and they were putting up a fight. The Wuftoom had spread themselves out so they had room to move and draw. Many were very good shots, and their streams were throwing the Vitflys with such force that many of them fell and didn't rise.

But there were still many more Vits than Wuftoom, and many Wuftoom had fallen. Evan saw a Vit land on a body and dig its fangs in, until another Wuftoom knocked it off and the Vit sank under the water. Another Vit dived, and the Wuftoom swung for it but missed. The Vit landed on the Wuftoom's head and dug its claws in, and the Wuftoom twisted in pain. Evan could not hear the Vit's screech and the Wuftoom's growl over the din, but he knew what they would sound like.

He shrank back a little. There was no fighting directly in front of the pipe, but if he dropped down, he would surely draw attention to himself.

It occurred to him that he could leave. He could go back home and see his mother. He could live with her, or at least near her, just like he'd once told Olen he planned to do. He'd find a way. Dig a hole for himself beneath his house. Eat human food if he had to. But if he did that, what would happen to Tret and the others? Tret would not leave *him* behind, he was sure of it. Even after the secrets Evan had kept, Tret would still save him.

He could not stand to think about it any longer, and with a deep breath he dropped legs first into the pipe. Without stopping to see if he was noticed, he ran to the nearest Wuftoom, who was fighting with his back against the wall. It was Rayden.

"Tret, Ylander, and Horg are in a small pipe up the crawler. They're badly injured! Tell everyone you see!"

"What happened?" Rayden growled.

"The Vits came up the hole," Evan answered. "Everyone else is dead. I put them in the pipe and came for help." The screeching of the Vits grew louder. "But we did drop the bomb afterward."

Rayden glared past Evan at the fighting beyond.

"Watch out!" Evan cried.

A Vit flew toward Rayden's head.

Evan swung at it, but it dodged. It flapped its wings and hissed, its eyes glowing bright yellow. Foul.

"You did this!" Evan cried. "You killed Master Olen! You killed Suzie!" He swung at Foul again, but again the Vitfly dodged.

Rayden smashed another Vit, and then another. But Evan had eyes only for Foul. He swung again.

"You are not a Wuftoom," Foul hissed. "You want them dead as much as we do."

"I don't!" Evan cried. "I *am* a Wuftoom!" He swung.

Foul danced away, just out of reach. "Your mother missssses you, *Evan.*" It gave a screeching chuckle. "Sssshe still cries." Facing Evan, it didn't see Rayden circle behind it.

Rayden's Feeder connected with Foul's hairy backside.

The Vit fell into the water with a splash.

Rayden reached into the water and pulled Foul out, his nub wrapped tight around Foul's body, holding its wings.

Foul opened its mouth wide and hissed, water dripping from its fangs.

"Brode is a Wuftoom," Rayden hissed back. "And you" — he screeched Foul's name — "are done." Rayden shoved Foul back underwater.

The Vit struggled and the water splashed.

Three Vits flew at Rayden's back.

Evan whacked one, but the other two got through. They landed and dug their claws in.

Rayden stood up, pulling the struggling Foul with him. He swirled around, growling, trying to dislodge the Vits.

Foul screeched, struggling against Rayden's nub.

Evan smashed one of the Vits on Rayden's back, then the other one. They both hung there, their dead claws still shredding Rayden's membrane.

Rayden shook wildly, trying to dislodge the dead Vits from his back. He dropped Foul.

Foul flapped its broken wings, just managing to lift itself above the water.

Evan lunged, wrapping his arm around the injured bug.

It dug its fangs into Evan's arm.

Evan screamed. It was even worse than in the Yellow Passage. But he hung on. He pushed Foul beneath the water.

Rayden collapsed into the water with a splash.

Foul struggled, but Evan didn't let go until its fangs loosened their grip. When the Vit had stopped struggling completely, he let it sink to the bottom, finally dead.

"Rayden!" Evan cried.

The old warrior was lifting himself out of the water. The dead Vits floated away, but more Vits were heading for them.

Evan raised his Feeder, holding his injured arm against his body. It stung like nothing he'd ever felt. It was hard to see anything, to feel anything except the pain.

Water hit him from two sides, tossing the Vits backward. There was shouting, Wuftoom voices. At first he didn't understand, but then the sound came into focus.

"Back!" they were shouting. "Go back!"

Evan threw his good arm around Rayden. Water flew everywhere around him, then stopped suddenly. As it cleared, he saw that a few Wuftoom were showering groups of Vits, trying to get them off those who were still standing. Evan turned toward the cave, supporting Rayden, whose legs weren't quite working right. He didn't know if he was hurting the old one worse, but he didn't have time to stop and think.

He heard screeching behind him, saw Wuftoom bodies in the water, felt the spray of water, and heard the continued yelling: "Go back! Go back!" He did not stop until he reached the waterfall and pulled Rayden through it into the cave.

More Wuftoom followed him, but not many. He held

Rayden's head up. It was too much like his last moments with Olen. He could not stand it.

"Master Rayden! Master Rayden, can you hear me?"

Rayden growled a little and his eyes began to glow. He looked up at Evan. "I have been clawed before and come out stronger," he said. But his voice was not booming and strong as it had been before. It was not the storyteller's voice.

"I'll get the ointment," Evan said, and he set Rayden against a set of blocks. He rushed to where he knew the medicine was kept. It was near the weapons. Everything the Wuftoom owned and needed to survive was all lined up among discarded blocks along a single wall.

Two others were already raiding the stores. They pushed a creature-skin jar toward him and rushed off without a word. Evan's eyes followed, and he saw a group of wounded propped against the front wall. He recognized Jordan as one of those helping them and his heart leaped, but he could not continue looking.

He dug in the cabinet for a needle and thread, like the kind that had been used on him. He didn't know what creature they were made from, but the needle was sharper and smaller than a Vit fang. At last he found it, and rolling the supplies in his good arm, he sloshed back to Rayden, sending the water flying.

Rayden was no longer awake. He had rolled a little onto his side but still maintained most of his shape.

"Master Rayden!" Evan cried. He dropped the supplies on the blocks and shook the old one with his good arm. "Rayden! Wake up!" There was no answer. "Please, Rayden!" Throughout everything, Evan had never wished so much that he could cry. He couldn't let another Wuftoom die. He just couldn't. He picked up the ointment and started rubbing it into Rayden's head. There were so many wounds on his head, arms, and back that by the time Evan was finished, Rayden's whole body shined with ointment.

The old one moved a little. It was so slight, Evan almost didn't believe it.

"Rayden!"

Rayden made a tiny little noise and moved again, ever so slightly.

"Master Rayden! It's me, Brode. I'm trying to fix you up. I'm going to sew you. Just hold still. You're going to be fine."

Rayden made no noise, but now he was visibly breathing. Evan didn't know how he was going to do it, since his right arm was useless. He poured what ointment was left onto it and rubbed it in with his left arm. There wasn't enough left to give it as good a coating as Rayden's back, but he already felt a little better.

Fortunately, the needle he had grabbed was already attached to thread. He decided he would just start with the very worst part of Rayden's back and do what he could. Then he suddenly realized what he could do. He was a Wuftoom. He could squoosh himself so small that he could travel through an ordinary bathroom pipe. Certainly he had more that was useful than just his arm.

Hope suddenly flooding through him, he sat down on the ground and raised his right leg to his left arm. As a Wuftoom, this didn't hurt a bit. Although he wasn't used to using it this way, he found that he could grab a piece of Rayden's membrane with his leg and pull it forward to meet the needle.

Some time later Master Gorti joined him. He was a little torn up himself and covered in pus from other worms, but he was alive. Evan thought he'd never been so happy to see anyone.

"This is good, young one," he said, and he began to help. An hour later Rayden's back didn't look pretty, but all the major holes were closed. Rayden had said nothing the whole time, but he was still breathing. His whole body pulsed slowly in and out.

"We will let him rest, young one," said Gorti.

Evan nodded, then suddenly remembered. "Master Gorti! Tret and Ylander and Horg are back near the dig. I left them in a small pipe."

Gorti motioned to Jordan, who slid over to them. He had a cut on his head that shone with ointment, but he looked otherwise well.

At first there had been others standing, but now the rest were sitting against the wall, gasping with the pain of various wounds.

Evan counted eight in total, nine if he counted himself. Twelve if all of the others lived. Out of a hundred. The gravity of it fell on him like the weight of the ceiling caving in. He could see it in Gorti's eyes as well.

Jordan clapped Evan with warmth, but a change had come over him. He was no longer excited and young.

"We will take the pipes," said Gorti. "It is too dangerous to go out through the water. The Vits may by lying in wait." Gorti led them to the vents at the back of the cave, where Tret, Suzie, and Ylander had taken him that first night.

They went a different way this time, to where the pipes were old and collapsed, where the sewage leaked out into the dirt and spread its stink. It was a roundabout way to travel, but they reached the crawler within an hour. Evan led the way to the pipe where he had hidden them.

Tret and Ylander were still alive, barely. The compressing had kept them from losing pus, and they had slept to save their strength. But Horg came out in a formless lump, and it was clear that he was dead. Jordan took Ylander, Gorti carried Tret, and Evan dragged Horg's body behind him with his one good arm.

THIRTY-THREE

WHEN THEY RETURNED, Rayden was awake, and those who could had gathered around him. Evan, Jordan, and Gorti dragged Tret and Ylander to the waiting Wuftoom, and the Wuftoom began to stitch Tret and Ylander the best they could.

"We must leave this area," said Rayden. It was not the storyteller's voice yet, but it was stronger. He was fully shaped against the blocks now. "Once, there were Wuftoom elsewhere. I do not know where they are or what has happened to them these many years, but we cannot stay here, a few among an unknown number of Vitflys. These are the only Vits I know of. If we run, we can escape."

"We have our waterfall," said Gorti. "Perhaps we should wait and build our strength."

Rayden shook his head. "The Vits can fly above the ground. They have strengths we did not know about before. They will find and destroy our water source."

The Wuftoom around him gasped. Evan pursed his lips and sucked air in. He had not had time to worry about that, but he knew Rayden was right.

"As soon as we are well enough," said Rayden, "we will go."

The others solemnly nodded agreement. There were none of the customary Wuftoom growls, no cheers or voices raised in fierce debate. All knew the strength of Rayden's logic. Tret lay in front of Evan, propped on a block. Jordan twisted the thread and stuck the needle in again. Tret did not wake.

Can you ever forgive me? Evan thought.

After three nights, there were only nine left. The two new dead ones were folded and laid gently with Horg and the few others they'd been able to salvage. The ceremony would be saved for later, when the group had escaped from this part of the sewers. The others were well enough to move, but some were still torn and shedding pus from wounds so large that the stitches couldn't hold them. Ylander was among the worst wounded, needing another Wuftoom to help him even onto his sleeping blocks.

Tret had not smiled since he had woken, though he led the preparations for their journey with stony resolve.

Rayden and Tret drew maps and plotted paths on membrane sheets, then scratched them out and started over. They argued and scratched, then argued more, and finally reached agreement on each point in turn.

Evan watched, helping to tend the injured when he could. His arm was healing well, but he felt useless among so much pain and death. Jordan and Gorti were the least injured, so they ventured out through the vents to scrape the pipes for water creatures.

To add insult to slaughter, the Vits had managed to remove their dead. Food was so scarce that Evan had only two bites in those three nights. Combined with the hunger from before the battle, it left him itchy, nervous, and unable to think.

On the fourth night, Tret and Rayden sat with Ylander and the worst wounded, and the rest gathered around.

"We must leave tomorrow night," said Rayden. "We have stayed here too long already. It is a wonder our hunters are still alive." He did not need to mention how badly they were all starved. "The young one and I have plotted a course. It will take us through the narrowest passages, the wettest ground. There are places where we must cross tunnels where Vits go, but they are as short as we could make them."

Tret sat next to Rayden, nodding as he spoke. He had never seemed so supportive of Rayden before. This new accord between them was so strange, it made their peril feel worse.

"We will each carry two packs," Rayden continued. "One as a weapon, and one for our fallen brothers." Rayden looked solemnly at each in turn. "We will plant them where they will be most useful. The time has come to raise our numbers faster than ever before."

The Wuftoom looked at each other, all except for Jordan, who had not been there for the story.

"I have been the one to caution against haste," said Rayden, "and even now I question the wisdom of making many at once, when the humans are likely to notice. But the young one has convinced me. If we do not make more quickly, we will all die. We will plant them as soon as we are far enough away."

When it was time to go to sleep for their last day, Evan approached Tret and Rayden, who were still whispering together, making their final plans. A large piece of membrane lay between them on a table of concrete blocks.

"You should sleep, Brode," said Rayden. "We have a long night ahead of us and many more."

Tret looked up at him with dull eyes.

Evan took a breath in. He had to say it. He had no choice. "Before we go, I need to say goodbye to my mother," he said. He did not look away but watched as their eyes glowed and their lips twisted into unreadable expressions.

Tret took such a deep breath that his body visibly expanded. Rayden showed nothing of what he felt.

"I don't think I'm going to forget," said Evan. "But I don't want to stay there. I want to go with you. But I promised I would say goodbye." What would they say? Would they even now keep him from going?

Rayden and Tret looked at each other, and some silent agreement passed between them.

"We were expecting you to say something like this," said Rayden. He ran a nub across the membrane, smoothing it. Evan could see it was a map.

"We cannot spare any of us to go with you, not with so many wounded. It is a dangerous proposition to go alone."

"I know that," Evan said, "but I don't have any choice. I have to go."

"Then that is your choice," said Rayden. "We will meet you here." Rayden extended his nub into a point.

Evan leaned over the table. The place Rayden pointed to was not on the maps he had seen before.

"We are here," said Rayden. He extended his other nub into a finger and pointed at a second spot.

Evan examined the second spot. That part he had seen before. The familiar territories spread out to the left on the map, back to the hunting passages. To the right, there were passages and caves that he had never known about.

"We have planned a night of rest here," said Rayden, tapping the first spot he had pointed to. "You must catch up with us before the day is out. We must leave the next night. We cannot wait longer for any Wuftoom."

Evan leaned in further, trying to study the membrane. How would he ever find his way?

"You can take this one," said Rayden. "We have two others."

Evan breathed out. He wasn't sure if he had breathed again since he had approached them. "Thank you, Master Rayden! Thank you, Tret!" Evan said. "I'll be there. I won't be late." He was about to turn away when Tret spoke for the first time.

"If you still love your mother, how can we be sure that the Vits won't use her again? How can we trust you?" His tone was quiet. Not accusing, just a question. Both Wuftoom watched him for an answer.

"I've already told her to leave," he said. "I'll make sure she leaves this town for good, and goes far enough so the Vits will never find her."

Tret and Rayden looked at each other, then turned back to Evan. "Is there anyone else they could use?" Tret asked.

A month ago the answer to this question would have shamed him. Now it lifted his heart. "No," he said. "I didn't have any other family or friends."

"Very well," said Rayden. Tret nodded and his lips untwisted a little. He began to roll the membrane map. He rolled it into a tube, then folded the tube until the map was just a tiny square. He held it out to Evan, and Evan took it.

"Go with care, Brode," said Tret.

Evan almost corrected him, told him that his name wasn't Brode, that he wanted to be called Evan, but he stopped himself. Tret had put up with a lot from him. He shouldn't push him any further. Besides, there was a part of him that wasn't sure. Was he really a Wuftoom now? Should he want to be called Brode? Did he?

Evan went back to his sleeping blocks, where Jordan had set up next to him. *No,* Evan thought, *not Jordan, Rutgi.* But Evan couldn't let Jordan go.

"What did Tret give you?" Jordan asked.

"It's a map," said Evan. "So I can find my way to meet you after I go see my mother."

Jordan gasped and pulled his lips in. "Brode, you can't go out there alone. It's crazy!"

"I have to," said Evan. He couldn't explain this to Jordan.

But Jordan didn't try to argue anymore. Instead, he put his nub around Evan and gave him a hard clap, squeezing into Evan's back. "Be safe, Brode. I don't know what I'd do if you didn't come back. I wouldn't even be here without you."

Evan sucked in his breath. "You know?"

"Of course," said Jordan. "I've meant to say thank you. I never would have gone near that field on my own."

"You . . . you're not sorry you're a Wuftoom?" Evan asked.

"Sorry?" asked Jordan. "Are you kidding? I was *meant* to be a Wuftoom. This is where I belong."

Evan looked down at the water. He knew the old Jordan wouldn't say this, but he also knew that Jordan was being sincere. Rutgi wasn't sorry he was a Wuftoom at all. And he really was Evan's friend.

"We mean it," said Ylander, sloshing up to them with help from Gorti. "Come back."

"Yes, Brode," said Gorti. "Master Olen would want that." Gorti unrolled an arm, revealing half of a recently dead Higger.

Evan stared at it. The sight of the creature brought all his hunger up.

"Go on, take it," said Gorti. "You haven't eaten anything in days."

Evan didn't want to take it, but he was too hungry. He ripped it from Gorti's arm and shoved it into his mouth, swallowing it after one bite. "Thank you," said Evan. He meant it more than he'd ever meant any thank-you in his life.

"Just come back," said Gorti.

Evan had never seen a Wuftoom hug before, but he didn't care. He threw his arms around Jordan, Ylander, and Gorti, squeezing all of them together. "I will," he said.

THIRTY-FOUR

EVAN ROSE EARLY, hoping to reach his mother's house at sundown. At least the most dangerous part of his journey would happen when the Vits should be asleep. He took only a Feeder. Others would take his packs, so they could be used in case he didn't make it.

He made his way quickly through the pipes and did not come across another creature. It should not have surprised him. Other creatures typically avoided Wuftoom. Yet there was something strange about the silence. Perhaps there had always been more creatures than Evan had seen, making noises he'd never noticed.

The thought made a chill pass through his flesh. The Wuftoom had always hunted these creatures, yet they had never fled before. As he pushed through the water, its sloshing reverberated as if it were iron on steel.

The bedroom was silent. Evan ignored the lifting of pressure, let his body do what it would. He knew now that he would not break apart, no matter how terrible he felt. He went straight to the boarded window and reached behind the painting. He pulled out a scrap of paper with a note written on it in his mother's hand.

"Dear Evan, I'll come back every night at nine. I love you. Mom."

Evan sat on the bed. He could go back into the pipes to wait for the hour before nine. He would not have to endure this pain. Instead, he went back to the window. The two-dimensional meadow and the fake blue sky stared back at him. Slowly, he took down the painting and set it aside. Now he was looking at bare boards. He slid his nubs behind them, flattening his arms so that the liquid of his body flowed. He spread them outward until some part of his arms covered most of the window, and he pulled.

The boards came off with a pop and pushed him backward, so that he fell on his back onto the floor. He hit his head on the end of the bed as he fell, but his Wuftoom body was not hurt. He thrust the boards aside and scrambled to standing again.

There was the backyard, just as he remembered it. With his new eyes, it looked in darkness close to how it had looked before in light. There were the dandelions; there was the oak tree. Even the rope ladder was still there. There was the street, the train tracks, the whole town spread out before him.

The sun had gone down now, but there was still too much light for Evan. His body wanted to shrink back, to jump into the bathtub and ride the pipe down into the safety of the darkness. His eyes burned like they were filled with sand. But he wanted to look. He might never see this view again, or any view above the ground.

A raccoon poked its nose out from behind the oak tree.

Soon, another raccoon's nose poked out. With his enhanced hearing, he heard their chittering. Light creatures. Creatures as different from him as sea bass were from insects, or more so. The raccoons took off running. The night wind whistled through the houses and whirred as it was set free into the street. Evan wished he could go out there, just one more time.

The bedroom door creaked open. His mother gasped and ran over to him. She threw her arms around him and squeezed. Out of instinct, he tried to pull away. He must be ugly. He must stink. But his mother only pulled him closer and began to sob.

Evan melted into her, his nubs melting into each other and spreading across his mother's back.

"You shouldn't have come back here!" he cried. "I could have found you. They might come back!"

"What if you didn't?" she sobbed. "What if I never saw you again?" She squeezed him tighter, and his malleable body squashed and twisted under her grasp.

"You have to leave now. You can't ever come back here. You have to leave this town. You have to go far away from here, so they'll never find you again. Neither one of us will be safe until you get far away."

"Come with me!" she sobbed.

"I can't," said Evan. "Look at me. I'm one of them now. I have to stay with them."

His mother pulled herself away, grasped his shoulders, and held him at arm's length. By the moonlight, she could see him. "How many others are there?" she asked.

Evan's body shook. His mother felt it, and it looked like she would cry again.

"There were a hundred. But now there are only nine. We're leaving so the Vits won't get the rest of us."

Now she did begin to cry again and pulled him closer.

"Mom, please stop. Let me tell you." And he told her everything. From stepping in the pink goo in the field to when Olen had come, to when he had changed, and everything that happened after. "I'm still not sure how I feel about it, but I have friends, a clan. They'll take care of me even though I'm different. I know they will. I have to stay with them."

His mother continued to cry, but her sobbing was less.

"Is it hurting you to sit here now?" she asked.

"Yes," he said, "but it's my last time to even see the outside. I can handle it a little longer." The bedside clock showed 3:00 a.m. Just a few more hours until sunrise.

They sat there together while the hours passed, sometimes talking, sometimes looking out the window together. Finally, the sky began to glow.

"I have to go now," he said.

His mother nodded.

"Mom, you have to promise to be happy. You can move on with your life. You can get married. You can have more kids."

She smiled a little. "I don't need any more kids."

"But you can have them if you want. You can do anything you want now."

She nodded again. They both knew it wasn't that simple, but there was no need to say it.

"You promise to be happy too," she whispered.

They held on to each other again for a long time. Then she followed him into the bathroom and watched as he lined himself up over the drain, melded himself together, and slid away.